# Moonbeams & Shooting Stars

## Discover Inner Strength and Live a Happier, More Spiritual Life

### GWINEVERE RAIN

Prentice Hall Press, New York

Most Prentice Hall Press books are available at special quantity discounts for bulk purchases for sales promotions, premiums, fund-raising, or educational use. Special books, or book excerpts, can also be created to fit specific needs.

For details, write: Special Markets, Penguin Group (U.S.A.) Inc., 375 Hudson Street, New York, New York 10014.

Prentice Hall Press
Published by The Berkley Publishing Group
A division of Penguin Group (USA) Inc.
375 Hudson Street, New York, New York 10014

First Prentice Hall edition / March 2004

Visit our website at www.penguin.com

Library of Congress Cataloging-in-Publication Data
Rain, Gwinevere, 1984 –
    Moonbeams and shooting stars / Gwinevere Rain.
        p. cm
    Includes bibliographical references (p.   )
    ISBN 0-7352-0348-2
    1. Spiritual life.  2. Teenage girls—Religious life.  3. Young women—Religious
life.  4. Goddess religion.  5. Witchcraft.  I. Title.
    BL625.9.T44R35  2004
    204'.4'08352—dc22
                                                                    2003063765

**THIS BOOK BELONGS TO:**

_____

**PURCHASED OR GIFTED TO ON:**

_____

**FROM:**

_____

✳

My Birthday (month, day, year): _____

Astrological Sign: _____

Favorite Colors: _____

_____

Name of My Best Friend(s): _____

_____

Name of Pet(s): _____

_____

Future Career Aspirations: _____

_____

_____

_____

Things I Want to Accomplish: _____

_____

_____

_____

## A MOONBEAM BLESSING

*Oh, luna's whisper of the twilight time*
*Enchant this book with my rhyme*

*Here and now a blessing of pages*
*In the name of ancient goddess sages*

*Where tender fairies of sun-kissed night*
*Dance beneath candles glowing bright*

*Moonbeam web and twinkle star*
*Forever near, never far*

*So be it now with love and laughter*
*Bless these pages till ever after!*

# Contents

# Acknowledgments

Blessings and thanks to my family and friends, whose energies contributed to this book in one form or another. To my mother for believing in my vision, my brother Chris for his long-distance support, and Maggie and Seetal, my two best friends, for the memories and laughter.

To M.R., whose inner strength is admired and guidance treasured. Forever remembered, S.C. for illuminating the path I follow. Author Patricia Monaghan for her helpful input on the goddess section.

To Christel Winkler, editor and friend, for embracing the concept and keeping it true. And finally, to the higher powers, my Goddess and God, whose love is divine and pure.

Thank you for your good vibes, compassion, understanding, and support. Many moonbeam hugs, Gwinevere Rain.

# Catch a Shooting Star on a Moonbeam Journey

ITHIN THIS BOOK you will be asked to search your heart and soul. Lined journal pages will aid you in this task, along with special exercises that work in conjunction with each chapter's theme. Use the guided section to voice your ideas, aspirations, and concerns.

Please realize that once you've penned your intimate thoughts, this book evolves into a personal diary, expressing who you are and the internal challenges you've experienced. Just as you wouldn't want them to read a regular journal, convey this same desire to your family and friends. With that said, try not to leave the book out on the coffee table for wandering fingers. Under your pillow and in a dresser encourage privacy and tend to be safe places.

To start your moonbeam journey, inscribe your name and fill out the pieces of information requested on the first page of the book. It's a great idea to keep this book for future use. By imprinting these personal statistics you'll align your energies with this book, thus allowing it to reflect your true self at this very moment. At some point, you may consider giving it to a younger sister. Maybe you'd like to save this book for yourself, so years down the line you'll have the chance to read who you were at this time in your life. Or maybe you'll want to pass it down to a child of your own someday!

# Preface

TEEN WOMEN ARE soft warriors in a complex world. I should know, I am one. With this book, I hope to invoke a different approach to teen life. *Moonbeams & Shooting Stars* isn't about boys, clothing, or makeup. It's about you and your innermost thoughts, hopes, and dreams.

Before we move on, I'd like to give a quick tour of what's to come. To start, chapter one, "Dance Upon a Moonbeam," is your compass, a guide leading to the inner you, a beautiful soul and lively spirit. The second chapter brings in the power of the moon, Lady Luna, and her changing phases. If you'll listen to her whisper, she will help you mold your life into something bigger and better. Change like the moon and be renewed.

In chapter three, "The Goddess Speaks," we visit the land of mythology and discover Goddess power. Midway though your moonbeam journey we'll go deep inside to explore your hurt and pain. Only when you truly hear your anguish will it loosen its hold on your heart.

"Catch a Shooting Star: Wishes, Hopes, and Dreams" is an outlet for conveying your deepest desires and setting goals. Chapter six covers the multifaceted topic of angels. We will look closely at these amazing celestial beings and the roles they play within our lives. Angels are guardians who shadow our every move—guiding, caring, and loving. Last, we leave off with the concept of rituals: meaningful ceremonies that reinforce a woman's inner power.

In closing, as you hold *Moonbeams & Shooting Stars* in your hands, I want you to feel your own pure power. Together we will tap into your soul source and find a beautiful spiritual person. There is a goddess in you—now it's time to meet her!

# Introduction

I AM GWINEVERE RAIN, a writer and fellow teen. I follow a unique path called Wicca. It is a nature-based religion that honors dual deities, a Goddess and a God. Although this book is created for every young woman regardless of faith, you will find some Wiccan ideology throughout the text. Mainly, my religion has taught me to believe in myself, my intuition, and the goodness in people.

I don't believe a person should claim superiority. We are all equals—each special in our own way. Whether or not you are religious, I hope you'll agree with me when I say that each being living on mother earth has a soul. That whispering soul is exactly what *Moonbeams & Shooting Stars* is going to seek out and embrace. We are going to work together and get in touch with the inner you.

As your "tour guide" on this magical journey, I'd like to take a few moments and let you know a little bit more about myself. I grew up in Long Island, New York, and now reside in Florida, also known as the Sunshine State. My first aspiration that I can remember was to be on Broadway, singing my heart out. Slowly over the course of time that dream faded—not completely, but to the point where I knew the odds weren't in my favor. I started to think of other careers, others things I wanted to be: a veterinarian because I love animals, a lawyer because I enjoy a good debate.

Then, with my creative imagination and pen in hand, I took a stab at writing. It fit in my life like a missing piece of a puzzle. So now books possess the better part of my life. You can often find me reading, writing, conjuring up stories or nonfiction ideas.

However, life for me hasn't always been easy. I've had my fair share of bullies, mean teachers, broken friendships, and disappointing romances. Yet through it all I've lived, learned, and grown as a person. I am aware that at my age I still have a lot to learn, but I believe it is important to share with you a few things I have learned in hope that they might be able to help you.

One of the biggest mistakes people make when the topic of "soul-searching" comes up is that they assume to be "spiritually in tune" you have to be introverted, boring, or fanatical. I don't consider myself to be any of those. There is also an assumption that if you believe in being beautiful on the inside you shouldn't care about the outside. I care about the inside and the outside; I wear makeup, do my hair, and paint my nails like many other females my age.

Being spiritually connected doesn't require you to give up anything—in fact, you might just gain a great deal more. I listen to myself; I flourish in knowing that it's okay to be different. I am young, I am beautiful, and I am in touch with who I am. And so are you. You're all of these things too. If you don't believe me even for the slightest second, then this book is for you. Welcome to your soul. I am Gwinevere Rain, your tour guide on this magical journey within

# Dance Upon a Moonbeam

## Embrace Your Soul

T SEEMS LIKE everywhere you turn, you'll find some mention of the words "soul" or "spirit." New Age things like yoga, aromatherapy, or crystals are prominently featured in magazines or on the evening news. Commercialism has tapped into people's minds, trying to sell products that are good for the "soul." Yet nobody takes the time to dissect the meaning or explain the soul's attributes and function in detail.

What is this "inner spirit," and how does it affect you as a teen woman? I am glad you asked! The soul or spirit is deep inside each of us. It is the very core of our being. This hidden and mysterious place is where our self-image, aspirations, and emotions are softly stashed.

If we lived in a perfect world, everyone's spirit would be happy, healthy, and nurtured. We would all find our bliss and live happily ever after. Unfortunately, our world is far from perfect, and more often than not the collective human soul is ignored. This sounds awfully depressing, but there is hope.

What can you and I do to change this? Actually, a lot more than you'd think. The first step is to get in touch with your own soul and then help others with your intuitive knowledge and creative mind.

In other words, look to your soul, and build up the internal power you already posses. Then, use that amazing energy to aid others. We are going into the core of all that matters. As a teen woman you are the embodiment of strength. You are a teen guru. Now, let's get to the fun part, discovering the power and majestic abilities of your own soul.

## ✳ The Wisdom of You

Creating a connection between the mind, body, and soul will be different for everyone because each individual needs to overcome his or her own obstacles. In the end, only you can open the path to your own self-awareness.

I tend to think of this self-awareness process as an opening or soul journey. Like every journey, the steps you take are equally as important as the destination. I have found that one of the best ways to start on this soul journey is to write. Scribbling down your thoughts, emotions, hopes, and dreams can bring life back into your spirit. With the everyday chaos, it is easy to push your emotions aside and stop listening to your intuition. Sometimes if you don't address important issues, you'll get a spiritual "block." As teenagers, we need to express ourselves and have our thoughts articulated, even if it is only transcribed in a personal journal.

When you write down your fears, you're voicing them, and then they inevitability become easier to deal with. By fears, I don't mean the fear of heights; I mean the emotional fears we fight with on a day-to-day basis: a fear of abandonment, a fear of not being accepted. Half the time when I write in my journal a fear will come out, and then I will sit back for a minute and say to myself, "I didn't know that was even in there." By *in there* I mean deep inside my soul. These mini-revelations are stepping-stones on my own soul journey.

At first, writing in a journal can be scary. That is why I have developed a system you'll find throughout this whole book. The system is composed of fun, interesting, soul-quenching journal exercises. For example, one exercise will ask you to write about a favorite childhood memory that's fun to think about, but other journal exercises will challenge you a bit, like naming your worst characteristics.

The point of these exercises? To find, release, and embrace "The Wisdom of You."

## ✳ Spiritual Tools

I once read in an article where the author claimed that taking a bubble bath once a week will soothe the soul. To be honest that suggestion bothered me, and after giving it some thought I realized why. It's because a bath is just that, a bath. Water in a tub. I am sure it made the author of the piece feel calm and happy, but could a few scented bubbles really make a firm, dynamic impact on a person's soul?

In my opinion, this is not possible. That is, unless you combine a bath with meditation, prayer, or journaling. These techniques have been used for years and none of them requires bath beads or warmed towels. Meditation, prayer, and journaling have several common links. They all require the user to concentrate, visualize, comprehend, and articulate. Why should a teen use these spiritual tools? Because they help you get in touch with your soul source. The very goal we are all seeking. I've personally latched on to journaling, so I put an emphasis on this technique. But for a few moments, let's look at the other two—meditation and prayer.

Meditation is when you find a quiet place to get comfortable and close your eyes. It almost sounds like taking a nap. However, after deeper analysis you'll see that isn't the case! Sure, relaxation is part of meditation, but so is visualizing.

When meditating, you visualize a serene place, a positive memory, or a future goal. That's a lot more than taking a nap! During meditation, concentration is important. Some people chant, whisper, or use deep breathing during meditation periods. If you are open to this technique, you might want to give those methods a try.

As mentioned above, prayer can also be used to get in touch with your inner spirit. You can pray to the higher powers or perhaps your inner goddess (more on this in chapter three). Prayers can be directed toward deceased loved ones or family members who are far away.

It's not how you pray, where your hands are kept, or if your head is tilted down, it's that you pray in the first place. A prayer can be shouted, whispered, or silent. The message can be simple, soft, complicated, profound, or meaningful. Prayer is as individual as the person giving it. So, let your intuition guide you during this soul-searching technique. If you're lost on where to begin, pray for love, pray for peace, pray for family, and, every once in a while, pray to say thanks.

*To start your meditation session, locate a quiet place and adjust your-self into a comfortable sitting position. Close your eyes, take a deep breath, and exhale slowly. Listen to your breathing and let your mind conjure up positive images. Focus on a special place, memory, person, or goal. Let your breathing go deeper, inhaling and exhaling at the pace where your body feels most comfortable. Do your best to con-centrate on the chosen image, but don't force anything. Once you feel your meditation is complete, return your breathing to normal, men-tally thank the higher powers, and slowly open your eyes.*

## ✴ Find Your Soul Source

Now that the soul has been defined and you've been introduced to various spiritual tools, the next step is combining that knowledge to help you find your soul source. Then you'll develop a way to continuously stay in touch with that spiritual energy and personal power.

The soul isn't like some internal organ; you can't take an X ray of its exact location. So, finding that inner spirit can at first appear to be complicated. Honestly, it is so easy to locate that all you have to do is draw upon a positive memory and you'll find it instantly.

Let's think together. Many of my positive memories revolve around friends and family. There were a few summers (when I was young) that my family would make an outing to the beach.

We would swim, build sand castles (or sand creatures), and of course, collect seashells. Once or twice I brought home starfish that had been washed on shore. How can I forget the sound of the waves, the flapping of kites, or the call of seagulls? As I write about my good memory, I smile, my mind visualizes the glistening ocean, and I feel calm, relaxed, and happy. Drawing on positive memories helps me to connect with my soul anytime.

JOURNAL EXERCISE—*Write one or two of your favorite memories. It could be something that occurred years ago or this past week. Try to stick with a positive moment, as there will be another chapter in regard to unpleasant past events.*

Aside from memories, another way to find your inner being is to draw on issues, people, and situations that are currently making you feel optimistic and blessed. The other day I bought a vanilla candle. Vanilla is one of those delightful scents that "speak to me." As silly as it sounds, I am grateful for my scented candle, and whenever I look at it, I smile. The little things in life bring me pleasure.

Sometimes when the day is wild and windy, the breeze picks up my spirits and consoles my inner being. I feel alive and vibrant. What about you? What positive, ordinary things bring a smile to your mouth and a musical rhythm to your heart?

JOURNAL EXERCISE—*Create a small list of current things, issues, or ideas that uplift your spirit and bring positive, beneficial energy into your life, i.e., an afterschool club or great book.*

After participating in these journal exercises, you probably feel a bit tingly inside. Good, that means they have worked! You've found your soul source and are now embarking on an amazing self-enlightening journey! Once you've opened your heart, that spiritual energy won't be blocked up; but like everything in life, it never hurts to add a little oil, do a little maintenance, and keep that door squeak-free. These journal exercises are like daily maintenance checks on your soul. They are beneficial for your creativity and emotional stability, as well as your heart and mind. The next stop on your soul journey: how to balance that youthful energetic spirit and protect your core being.

## ✳ Balance Your Spirit

Your spirit likes attention. It thrives on journaling, meditation, and prayer. Yet sometimes to create a little balance you have to look outside of yourself and pay attention to someone else's soul. Who hasn't had a friend that begins every sentence with the word "I"? There is only so much a person can put up with, and "I" statements can become boring pretty quickly. So, what does this have to do with your soul? Everything!

Taking good care of your spiritual center is important. However, to balance your soul, going outside of yourself and reaching out to others is a must! How do you make an impact on someone's soul? There are countless ways! You don't even have to inform them you're on a quest for "spiritual balance"; just do something small and kind from the heart. As a little piece of advice, I suggest that you try to stay away from pushing your beliefs on other people. There are other ways to help without bringing intense political or religious beliefs into the picture.

For example, you know that extremely quiet girl in the back of the class? Talk to her—even a warm smile and a hello goes a long way. Get out of your "me" routine and make an effort to be kind for one day; you'll see a big difference. Balance is the key: help others, help yourself. You don't have to single-handedly feed all the homeless people in your town—that's not the goal. The goal is to bring comfort to someone who needs it, a kind word to someone who's ignored, or a friendly gesture of appreciation. It's the little things that go a long way. I believe in karma; what energies you send out into the world, you'll eventually get back. Now that's balance!

JOURNAL EXERCISE—*Write down three positive things you can do to make a person's day brighter and better. Throughout this upcoming week make an effort to follow through on those ideas.*

# ✳ Protect Your Spirit

How do you protect something so sacred, so important, and so . . . invisible? Well, you start by recognizing the outside influences that are harmful to your spirit and work from there.

High school is not an easy place for your inner spirit to feel blissful and nurtured. In truth, sometimes high school can be an extremely hostile and soul-wrenching environment. Yet your parents still push you out the door in that direction.

It's not the school building itself that does a number on your soul, it is the negative energy you may encounter on a day-to-day basis. There will always be that rude and annoying person who tries to make your life miserable. I wish I had some magical words of advice to make that all go away, but I don't. I can, however, provide you with some coping mechanisms that will help keep you and your inner spirit from being drenched in negativity.

Let's begin before you even get to school! At home, in your room, before you head out the door to start your day, seize a moment for yourself. Close your eyes, take a few deep breaths, and imagine yourself surrounded by a ball or mist of white light. This handy technique is called visualizing. The color of white symbolizes purity, goodness, protection, and possibilities. Whenever you're stuck in a negative situation at school just visualize that white energy around you. After a few weeks of using this simple tool, you'll wonder how you ever survived without it!

Another step in protecting your soul source involves controlling your environment or, in some cases, the people you hang around with. I am not trying to tell you who to be friends with and who to avoid, but the people you surround yourself with do a serious number on your soul. Positive energy is beneficial; negative energy is totally destructive.

Gossip is draining, drugs will ruin your life, and controlling boyfriends can damage you as well. I believe that you're smart enough to know the difference between what's healthy and what's not. But sometimes you need to remind yourself where the boundaries lie.

Reevaluate your environment and the people you socialize with. Are they doing more harm than good? Do you feel drained of positive energy when you hang out with them? Have you ever felt scared while in their company? If you've answered "yes" or "maybe" to any of these questions, it's time to do some serious thinking about your so-called friends!

On the flip side of this equation, school may be the place you go to for an escape. An escape from your family and distressing home life! You can't trade in your family, break up with them, or call it quits. For the most part, you're stuck with them.

The keys to surviving siblings and parents without going crazy are learning to compromise on important issues and finding time for yourself. Compromising doesn't always mean giving in and following "orders," or giving up your say in a situation. It means talking out your feelings, considering the other person's side of an issue, and then, together, finding a common ground. There is a saying that goes something like this: "Pick and choose your battles wisely." Meaning some things are worth fighting about while others aren't! Use your intuition to weed out the important things from the not-so-important ones. If your sister borrows your shirt, deal with it; if she breaks your science project on purpose, then you've got a right to be upset!

Remember to set aside a little "me" time every day. Reserve a few minutes for yourself away from everyone in your family, because sometimes a girl just needs to breathe.

An uncomfortable family situation might not even involve you directly, such as your parents fighting with each other. However, if it's going on in your home, believe me when I tell you it has an impact on your life and soul. A healthy marriage will have fighting from time to time; it's a way for some people to air the issues. Unfortunately, some parents fight so much it makes the kids feel really uncomfortable and hurt. The thing to remember is that more often than not, the parents probably don't realize how much their negative energy is affecting their children.

Depending on your situation, you may have to bring this issue to their attention and tell them how you feel when they fight. Don't be afraid to speak from the heart. Letting them know how you feel gets your voice heard and releases you from that yucky feeling inside, the one that you get when you feel you haven't been heard. It will also shed some light on the situation at hand. Then, the next time your parents fight, hopefully they'll hear your voice inside their head, urging them to stop.

Compromising, taking time for yourself, and being vocal are all great coping tools for the home life, but don't be afraid to pen your feelings out too. Writing about issues gives you more control. I know when I feel totally trapped and powerless, that inch of control makes all the difference!

JOURNAL EXERCISE—*Use this section to express any issues in regard to your home or school environments that might be stressing you out.*

# A Stone's Throw Away –
## a Ritual for Your Soul

This ritual is simple but meaningful. It's designed with the direct purpose of helping you become more in sync with your soul and spiritual center. All it requires is an open mind and something you see every day that can be found around the house, literally.

On a Friday afternoon, take a short walk by yourself or with a close friend. Think about something positive (maybe one of the memories you penned down earlier in the chapter) or talk casually with your friend. After a few minutes when there is a lull in your conversation or thought, ask your soul to open its doors with this chant:

> Sweet serenity soul of mine,
> Open bright, shine with light.

If you haven't already, stop walking, close your eyes, and take three deep breaths. When you open your eyes, glance toward the ground and pick up a stone that calls to you. It can be itty-bitty, or heavy and hard. Bring it with you and return inside.

Once indoors wash the rock in cool water. Dry it well and bring it back to your room. Find a comfy place to sit and roll the stone between your palms. After a few seconds it will probably start to be warm from the friction. Stop rubbing the stone, but hold it tightly in your palms. Softly open your hands to reveal the stone and blow on it with three deep breaths, and say this poem aloud or silently in your head:

Stone of Earth, dirt
Cleansed by Water, rubbed with warmth,
I breathe my breath of life upon you,
Air sent with harmony's message,
Message received.

The ritual is done. Keep the stone is a safe place.

## Ritual Afterthoughts

(only read this once you've completed the ritual above)

You may think this ritual of selecting a stone is a bit odd. Once you learn the symbolism behind the ritual, you might not think so anymore. The ritual starts out by getting you adjusted in nature, thinking positive thoughts. Next, you're asked to open your soul and let your intuition pick a rock.

What makes you think that you picked it? Couldn't fate have picked the earthen rock? Or maybe the stone picked you?

The washing, rubbing, and breathing in conjunction with the stone brings together the four elements—Earth (the stone), Water (cleaning the stone), Fire (remember the friction?), and Air (your three deep breaths). Each of these elements is essential to your everyday life. Sometimes we take things for granted, but these elements are at the core of our very needs.

After the ritual, you might find yourself thinking about the stone, its color and shape. Your hands still remember how the stone felt dancing between your palms. Performing this ritual on a Friday is significant because that day of the week is astrologically ruled by Venus. Both the planet and Roman goddess influence love, self-love, and serenity. Most Fridays are lazy as people pause for the weekend ahead.

Even though the stone came from outside, in the dirt, for a few moments you embraced its magnificence. Isn't it time that you do the same for your own soul? Don't you deserve to be cared for and loved? Take the rest of the day for yourself and listen to your heart's message and voice.

CHAPTER   TWO

# Welcome Change
## Moon Wisdom and Phases

IN THE SUMMER, you'll often find me taking nighttime walks with my mother. A little while ago out on one of those strolls, I looked up and saw the moon gazing down. I remember thinking, What exactly is it about the moon that intrigues me? I don't believe I'll ever fully know the answer to that question, but I do have a few guesses. It is milky white, softly beautiful, and simply breathtaking. It follows me wherever I go, as if urging me in the right direction.

Unlike the harsh sun, that elegant moon—the goddess of the night—doesn't blind my eyes or burn my skin. She is there among the stars, illuminating the sky with her long, tender rays. Her glow invites, and despite what others may say, I still see a friendly smiling face in the moon. The sun gives us light, but the moon . . . the moon gives us love.

Within this chapter we'll study the moon, not as some rock in the sky, but as a transcending figure in our lives. Ancient people, civilizations thousands of years ago, used to believe the moon was a powerful deity. Our moon is symbolic of many treasures. Yet so often her energies are ignored. Together, we'll tap into her energy force and learn some fun tricks to harness those powers.

JOURNAL EXERCISE—*On this page, write down your favorite nighttime and moontime memories. Do you have memories of the moon from youth? Catching fireflies with childhood friends? Can you recall barbeques or family gatherings during the summer months that went on long into the night?*

_____

_____

_____

_____

_____

_____

_____

_____

_____

_____

_____

_____

_____

_____

_____

_____

_____

_____

# ✳ Use the Moon to Create Change

The moon drifts night to night, effortlessly changing from one phase to another. Her power is mystifying. I believe it is possible to use those changing energies in our lives. After all, who can't pinpoint an everyday situation that they'd like to change? Or a unique challenge they'd like to tackle? The moon, via her changing ways, tells us that change is a positive transformation. You don't have to be stagnant and take whatever comes your way.

At times, teens can feel change is useless because many believe they lack control within their lives. True, parents or guardians are there to help you along the path, but ultimately daily choices shape your present situation and future. It may be hard to fathom at first, but you are in the driver's seat at all times. No matter your age, you have the power to shape and mold your own life, present and future. So, if you feel something isn't going right, maybe it's time to take a different turn and invite change in for a little redecorating.

Change can show itself in subtle ways. For instance, nature is changing all around us every day. Half the time we barely acknowledge the falling of leaves during the autumn season. Worms cocoon and turn into butterflies. The sun rises and sets. Nature appears still, but if you look closely, it rarely remains the same.

Over the next few pages we are going to take a look at the moon, "the supreme queen of change," and see how you can tap into her energies via each specific moon phase and adapt that lunar change into your life.

For change to occur, you've got to identify your challenges and overcome them with a nudge, a push, and a heavy bout of persistence. Throughout this chapter, with the help of upbeat journal exercises, I will aid you in this task. Change seems at first a little scary, but if you're willing to take a small risk, things might turn around and alter your life for the better.

## New Moon

*I Spy.*
The new moon can be found when no moon is visible or you can see a tiny crescent in the sky. When the new moon crescent appears, it looks like a backward letter *C*.

*Energy.*
The new moon's subtle vibration yields beginnings and a fresh outlook. It's a starting point for new ventures.

*In Relation to You.*
The new moon is perfect for change! During this phase it is the best time to go out in search of a new job. If you're looking for a fresh start or beginning, new moon energy can most certainly help. Join a club at school or take up a sport you love. It's a time to "plant seeds" in any venture. Save your money so it may grow throughout the weeks and months ahead.

JOURNAL EXERCISE—*Write down three aspects of your life in which you're looking to start something new—like starting a friendship. How can this beginnings phase help you in your life?*

# Waxing Moon

*I Spy.*
When the waxing moon appears in the sky, it looks like the letter
D. The waxing moon gradually increases in size as the nights pass.

*Energy.*
The waxing moon's power centers around growth and increase.
Its positive energies allow us to draw in, build, and expand.

*In Relation to You.*
The waxing moon phase is the best phase to "get things done." If
your grades are less than stellar, work with this moon phase to
change them. Look within and pay attention. The waxing moon is
as much a time of inner reflection as outer action. Think positive
and work with the harmony of this moon time.

 JOURNAL EXERCISE— *Create a list of five inner qualities you love
about yourself. Read them every night before you go to bed during the next
waxing moon phase.*

# Full Moon

*I Spy.*
The full moon occurs when you are able to view the full face of the moon.

*Energy.*
Rapid running positive energy. The full moon projects the highest concentrated vibrations of any phase.

*In Relation to You.*
The full moon is my favorite moon phase! Moon power climaxes and creates an uplifting atmosphere. Its energy is very multipurpose, but it's the perfect night for a romantic date. If you're single and a homebody, make plans with your friends. Get together, have fun—your bonds will strengthen.

JOURNAL EXERCISE—*If I had to describe the full moon energy in two words, they would be "power" and "possibility." Make a list of your future goals both large and small. Dream of the possibilities; they might just come true.*

# Waning Moon

*I Spy.*
When the full moon decreases in size, the waning moon phase comes into play. It looks like the letter *C* in the sky.

*Energy.*
The waning moon signifies releasing, decreasing, and banishing. The vibration of this moon phase focuses on letting negative energy move out of your cosmic space.

*In Relation to You.*
Clean out your closets, rearrange your bedroom—this is a perfect time to get rid of the stuff you don't want in your life. This banishing process also includes nixing bullies, negative thoughts, bad habits, and unpleasant memories.

JOURNAL EXERCISE—*The most important changes you need to make in your life involve getting rid of things that make you unhappy. Take your time, grab the courage, and write. Who or what hurts your soul?*

# ✳ Big Change

Sometimes a big change is needed. A few years ago my mother and I moved from New York to Florida. We sold all of our furniture and flew down with some suitcases, a few boxes, and our dog. It was a big but necessary change. Generally speaking, other "big changes" include switching high schools, getting your first car, or breaking off a long-term relationship.

These changes aren't small, like deciding to join the track team—they can be life altering and sometimes scary. Changing a comfortable pattern in your life takes some getting used to. New schools involve making new friends. Your first car makes the world seem at your fingertips. The breakup of a relationship is a time of both transition into single life and mending a wound.

Change may cause excitement, fear, or doubt, but it's important to remember that change is necessary for us to grow and evolve. We expand our mind when we are challenged. Once obstacles are overcome they mold you into someone who has a history, who has triumphed and ultimately gained knowledge from her experience.

If you reach a point in your life where change becomes necessary and choices need to be made, pray, and converse with family and friends. But follow your heart and intuition. They will rarely let you down. And remember, sometimes it helps to be like the moon . . . and change.

# ✳ Combating Fear

I know what you're thinking. I've heard the saying too: "easier said than done." That pretty much sums up the fear aspect we all face when trying something new or different. A lot of my suggestions look good on paper, but I'll admit it's hard to take that first step. For you woeful people, I developed a "shed the light on it" journal exercise.

On the next blank journal page, you're going to write down the fears and obstacles that come between you and your goals. After all, the only way to get what you want is to identify the challenges and then seek out some way to eliminate them. Although I can't help you with the elimination part, I can tell you that I found persistence to be a good friend. It's right up there with intuition and positive inner qualities, which are "must haves" in life.

JOURNAL EXERCISE—*Before you start, you'll need two different colored pens (preferably black and red) for this exercise. First, outline your goals with your black pen. You might want to check back and see what you wrote under the full-moon-phase journal exercise. With every goal, make note of at least one obstacle that prevents you from directly obtaining your final desired result. Continue on with each aspiration.*

*It may take some time to come up with a mission and an obstacle, but you know yourself well. Inevitably, you're the only one getting in the way of that achievement. An intense thought, but true.*

*Next, using your red pen, circle the goal (make sure you can still read it) and cross out your challenge (again, make sure it's still legible). Do this with each goal and obstacle, respectively. By circling your goal, you are symbolically telling the universe, "This is what I want." By crossing out the com-*

*plication, you are symbolically stripping its power. The purpose of this act? You're letting the world know that your fears and challenges don't own you.*

Take a moment, glance at the page, and reflect. It's a good idea to close the book and do something else now, letting those goals and obstacles leave your mind. As a follow-up, over the course of the next few weeks, work hard to overcome the challenges in real life as they come up. It may help to visualize yourself crossing them out in your mind.

## ✳ Start Anew Too!

Every month the moon rejuvenates itself, casually moving from one phase to the next. Eventually, Lady Luna returns to a new moon once again. As you have already read, the new moon's energies are for beginnings and fresh starts. Why can't we also have an automatic and routine new beginning? The answer is, we can! We can tap into the new moon's power and utilize it each and every month as a fresh standpoint.

Each of the twelve months of the year has a new moon. Along with the full moon phase, the new moon is often marked on commercial calendars. By noting which day the new moon falls on each month, you'll have the opportunity to use that energy and start fresh. During this time it is important to put bad days in the past, mend rifts in friendships, and cleanse your mind of negativity. Start with a clean slate; this quick mini-ritual can show you how!

## Mini-Ritual for the New Moon

Perform this mini-ritual in the morning, afternoon, or night of the new moon. Go to a sink and turn on the faucet. Run a cool stream of water. Take three pinches of salt in the palm of your hand and start to rinse your hands. Say this chant aloud or in your mind:

Water is purity,
Salt is sea,
New moon, fresh energy.

Dab the water on your pulse points and make the conscious decision to start fresh and think positive from that moment on. When you feel that you're ready to embark on your new start, turn off the water and find something fun to do!

In conclusion, every woman's connected to the moon, so take comfort in her flowing power and amazing strength. Try drawing on the moon's positive functions and molding them into your life. After you try it a few times and notice results, you'll be glad you did.

Change is a powerful occurrence; you can't always stop or block its impact on your life. If you allow change to flow in and out, you'll learn lessons with every turn, which is a good thing, if you let yourself be challenged!

When you need a little rejuvenation, try out this cool moon ritual for confidence.

## MOON RITUAL FOR CONFIDENCE

**MOON PHASE:**

New or waxing

**SUPPLIES:**

This book, a pen, one lemon (cut in half), sugar, a glass of water, a mud mask, and a white or pink candle

**FOR BEST RESULTS:**

Perform ritual in pj's and slippers

On the night of the new or waxing moon, grab some time alone in the kitchen. Lay out your supplies on the table. Squeeze the lemon juice out of both halves into a glass and scoop out all the seeds with a spoon. Place the seeds on a paper towel and dry them well; you'll be using these a little bit later.

Pour water into the glass, sugar to taste, and add some ice. Sneak into the bathroom, apply the mud mask, and travel back to your setup area.

Light your candle, open the book, and enjoy the lemonade. Sweep up the lemon seeds you've set aside and place them in your hand. Imagine yourself happy, confident, and blissfully content.

Once you're done with the visualization, put the seeds down and count them out. How many did you find in that lemon? Let's say you found eight seeds. Using this number as an example, write down in your journal eight characteristics of someone strong, confident, and loving.

Wait, hold on! Is your mask done? Mine is. Okay, run and take it off and come back.

Now that you are beautifully refreshed, let's get back to this ritual! Take a look at the characteristics you wrote down, and check off each and every one that applies to you. I know you must have related to a bunch, because you are one strong person who is full of love and passion. All young women are.

This ritual is done; you can sit down, relax, drink more lemonade, and read a little. But before you go, let me tell you something you may not have realized about this ritual.

1. The moon's energies relate to this tangy fruit. Meaning, lemon properties correspond with the moon. So, you could say lemons are "moon food."

2. The seeds represent fertility, which is connected to you because all women posses procreative energies.

3. To realize your own beauty, you sometimes have to imagine the qualities that make someone beautiful and apply them to your own life.

4. If you did this ritual during the right moon phase (new or waxing), your self-confidence and inner love will grow and shine all week for others to see.

5. When life gives you lemons . . . make lemonade!

~~~~~~~~~~~~~~~~~~~~~~~~~~~~~~~~~~~~~~~~~~~~~~~~~

Enjoy your night; you deserve it!

JOURNAL EXERCISE—*Use this section during your moon ritual to list characteristics of someone who is strong, confident, and loving.*

_____

_____
_____
_____
_____
_____
_____
_____
_____
_____
_____
_____
_____
_____
_____
_____
_____

# The Goddess Speaks

## Ancient Power

W HEN I WAS LITTLE, I would sit with my mother on the steps in our house and she would read me Greek myths. The mythology books would show beautiful pictures and tell enchanting, heroic tales of the ancient gods and goddesses. Often our dog, Dusty, would sit behind us and listen for a spell too. I remembered the myths so clearly throughout the years that when we were assigned a book to read in seventh grade containing the Greek myths, I already knew the characters and vividly recalled the stories in my mind.

Who could forget the magic of the Olympic gods? They controlled the world: Zeus, the weather; Poseidon, the sea; Demeter, the land. The moon and sun were thought to be actual gods. If the ancient Greeks had a problem, they'd call to a particular god to fix it: Hephaestus was the god of metal smith, Aphrodite would help your love life, Apollo was a musician, and Artemis would aid you in the hunt. In ancient Greece, there was a god or goddess that ruled every aspect of life.

This was how the ancient Greeks related to the higher powers. They assigned them stories and character traits. Some were noble and strong, others refined and dignified. They also needed a way to explain questions that plagued them. Why did it flood? Their answer—because the sea god, Poseidon, was angry!

Our modern life seems so different from that of the ancient Greeks. We live in the age of technology, where science explains the mysterious. We know when it might rain or snow because the meteorologist on the TV tells us in advance! So we relate to the powers of deity on a spiritual level, in times of grief, and less in the sense of "Goddess, help me with the hunt, so I may feed my family."

Everyone has a different perspective on the higher powers. Some believe in one superior god, some cultures not only have a god but also demigods, other people choose not to believe in a god at all! I believe in both a goddess and a god. In my mind, I see a balance, yin and yang, masculine and feminine. If nature consists of male and female creatures, and humans come in male and female forms, then why isn't divinity both as well?

You might not agree with me on this point. That's okay and perfectly fine, but I do hope you'll agree with me on my next point. Deep inside, down to our very core being, each teen woman has a little bit of Goddess power. Maybe it's left over from the ancient people's strong polytheistic (multiple-god) belief, but to connect with something, you must first have something inside that invokes the connection. If you've ever heard of the theory "like attracts like," you understand what I mean. To relate to a god or goddess, you must first have a small part of them already within you. Just like children have similar DNA to their parents, humans have the spiritual DNA of deity soaked into our minds, bodies, and souls.

Ancient cultures around the world believed in the divine feminine power. Many years ago it was common to worship a goddess: the Chinese called her Kuan-Yin, the Irish named her Brigid, the Norse/Germanic people honored Freya, and the Egyptians worshiped Isis, "the Goddess of 10,000 names." Each group honored their goddess in a special way, some with rituals under the full moon, others with hymns, songs, and poems. Temples were created in their names, prayers whispered, and mythic stories passed down through each and every generation. In ancient societies a goddess figure was as important as a god. The two worked side by side.

Contemporary Goddess worship is slightly different than that of the ancients. Today people show respect for Her by lighting candles, gazing at statues, or meditating on a particular goddess. It might not be as prominent in society, but a belief in the Goddess exists and it is coming back with vigor and passion.

Modern Goddess celebrations don't require large temples, for we know that the Goddess is never far away. She resides in the earth, Her energies are in sync with the moon, Her soft eyes are the birds flying above. She communicates with us, through us, in Her own unique way. The Goddess's love, passion, and kindness are found not only in nature but within ourselves. Each person has Her divine enchanted spark tucked neatly away within our spiritual center. It's our job to find that power and use it!

She is within you, aching to be acknowledged, yearning to be set free.

Within this chapter, by utilizing classic mythology, you'll find a more intimate view of the Goddess. To start, look at three prolific Greek goddesses: Aphrodite, Artemis, and Athena. Then we'll analyze how you can relate to these images.

# ✳ Aphrodite

Aphrodite is the Greek goddess of love and lust. Due to the changing attitudes of the ancient Greek culture she became a very complex character. There are even two versions of her birth! Homer, the famous author and poet, said she was the daughter of Zeus and Dione, but the more popular theory states that she rose from the foam of the sea onto the island of Cyprus.

Aphrodite had torrid love affairs with other Olympic gods and even entered a few mortal romances, although in truth she was tricked into those by Zeus. Interestingly enough, Aphrodite was a mother, but she wasn't personified as the "motherly type." This goddess was portrayed as a beautiful, lust-driven deity, who at times had a nasty jealous streak.

Regardless of how many power trips she embarked on, Aphrodite did put her energy to positive matters. She was, after all, the goddess of love! With a golden apple or her "magic belt," Aphrodite would bestow her power of love upon many gods, mortals, and even animals. The ancient Greeks designed amazing temples in her name. Then seekers would travel to the temple with an offering. They came to Aphrodite's place of worship for help in regard to matters of the heart and promoting a successful love life.

## Aphrodite in Your Life

Some teens relate to Aphrodite: beautiful, popular, and desired by young men. You've probably figured Aphrodite and her teen counterpart have it all, right? Well, like Aphrodite, sometimes flirtatious females gain an unfavorable reputation. And unless you are a real goddess, youthful beauty won't last forever. Aphrodite's good points are confidence and compassion. She is an all-around dynamic goddess. How can you tap into Aphrodite energies and empower yourself with her positive character traits? Discover her passion, love, and spunk, then reclaim those qualities as your own!

Use the following poem to jump-start this process. Say the invocation whenever you feel the need to be rejuvenated with Aphrodite's positive attributes.

**APHRODITE'S RED ROSE INVOCATION**
*Aphrodite, goddess, passion and power*
*I call to you, for you, of you*
*Sea foam, gold, and glitter*
*Mystic eyes, strong and confident*
*Bring within—the red rose*
*Surround me, treasured beauty*
*I take inside, Aphrodite*
*She is me.*

# ✳  Artemis

Artemis is the Greek goddess of strength, the keeper of wild animals, a midwife and huntress. She was said to carry a bow and a quiver filled with silver piercing arrows. Even though this goddess assisted in childbirth, Artemis was an eternal virgin. She roamed the forest with a band of nymphs, avoiding male mortals and killing any of them who came upon her group.

Artemis was one of the most beloved goddesses of Greece, honored in rituals and worshipped as the moon. She lived so closely with nature that when in danger, she'd shape-shift into a bear or deer. Her warlike stance attracted the eye of a mysterious group of warriors called the Amazons. They claimed Artemis as their own, worshipping her as their patron deity.

Her image was contradictory because the ancient Greeks blended several local goddesses into her personification. Artemis became a loving, nymphlike huntress flashing through her domain, the Greenwood, shooting arrows that never missed their mark. Yet at the same time, she saved pregnant animals from hunters seeking prey. This lovely, youthful goddess claimed the title "Lady of Wild Things."

## Artemis in Your Life

Artemis is strong and powerful, yet giving and loving all at the same time. She is the embodiment of today's feminist, an enchanting warrior. Her qualities are numerous, but Artemis and teens who strongly relate to her energy often neglect to put themselves first. If you're taking care of others, fighting for a cause, or leaping over boundaries and obstacles, then your needs fade into the background. Don't forget to set some personal time aside for yourself and listen to your soul.

Use the invocation below to tap into Artemis's strength and vitality.

**ARTEMIS CALL**

*Call yonder to the Artemis moon*

*Nymph in the Greenwood Forest*

*Fly by night shooting silver arrows*

*Drumbeat fast, vitality*

*Worship, praise be, Artemis call*

*I scream, strength!*

*Into me, I yearn, I become*

*I scream, strength!*

*Artemis call*

*Artemis call down*

*Down to me*

*I am Her, She is me.*

## ✳ Athena

Athena is the Greek goddess of the arts, craft-making, wisdom, and war. She is also an agricultural goddess, overseeing farms and domestic work.

Athena's birth was rather strange and unique. She was said to have sprung from the head of Zeus, fully grown, wearing a suit of armor. Her warlike capabilities combined with wisdom and intellect proved to be very useful. This protectress and defender would aid young men in battles, leading them to victory. However, unlike her half brother Aries, Athena wouldn't wage war for entertainment.

This virgin goddess is dual natured, appealing to warriors as well as domestic women. Athena's softer side made her extremely popular among artisans, poets, writers, and painters. She became a woman's deity, ruling domestic crafts, the spindle, the pot, and the loom. She also presided over music, dancing, and even the invention of popular musical instruments.

Athena was a multifaceted goddess loved so much by her ancient people that the deity was honored with a city in her name: Athens, Greece.

## Athena in Your Life

Athena pulls off being a warrior, but also stays smart and virtuous. She can be seen as the "smart girl" in school, the brain of the pack, but also that teen woman who "keeps it together" by making plans instead of rushing empty-handed into a situation. The downside of an "Athena personality" is a tendency toward overworking. Do you really need to study for finals in February? Stop pressuring yourself! Use your smarts in a positive, fun way like joining the debate club!

Utilize this invocation when you feel the need to call upon Athena's mind power and warrior persona.

**ATHENA'S WARRIOR PATH**

*Athena weaving*

*Owl perched still*

*I pray to thee*

**Woman**

*Inventive passion*
*Athena, stand tall with victory*
*Follow the warrior path*
*And look within*
*For She is me.*

#  The Triple Goddess

One way of "sorting out" the goddess images is by placing them in a type of age category. The young goddess is adventurous, wild, and free. She has a fiery spirit and claims the title "maiden." The maiden goddess appears in the forms of girls, teens, and young women. She is youthful and bouncing with energy. When I picture her in my mind, I see her as a passionate spirit running through a forest.

The "mother" goddess is more adult. She represents fruitfulness, responsibility, and maternal love. She is the center of family. Her energies are those of healing, renewal, and manifestation. I envision the mother goddess holding a baby in a blanket by a rapidly flowing stream.

The mature goddess is often referred to as a "crone." She may not appear youthful, but her mind can still tap into the memories of her maiden past and learn from those powerful experiences. The crone goddess is filled with wisdom and advice. She is strong in mind, taking on burdens, solving or banishing problems. Her past experiences are never taken for granted. I see the crone on top of a tall hill, reflecting on the past and contemplating the future.

I love the symbolism and strength behind the triple goddess aspect, but it's hard for a teen to relate. When would someone feel the need to get in contact with a crone? She can at first seem intimidating, but what if we changed the word *crone* into *sage*? No longer is she unreachable. A sage goddess is warmer, friendly but still wise and intelligent.

The mother archetype might remind you of being told to "clean your room" or "do your homework." But a *nurturing goddess* might give you more comfort, especially if you need additional compassion in your life.

The maiden goddess is probably easier to relate to than the crone goddess. When would you need to call upon a maiden goddess? Do you seek advice from a friendly, impartial ear? Someone who won't judge you but knows you at the same time? Then it sounds like you need a sister . . . a *sister goddess,* that is!

In the next few pages we'll examine the triple goddess figure—maiden, mother, and crone—but with a small spin on the topic. After all, it is so much easier to relate to a sister goddess, feel love from a nurturing goddess, and take advice from a sage advisor. Hopefully, these goddess figures will expand your awareness of the feminine deity power.

Allow yourself to find the energy of the Goddess. Just like Aphrodite, Artemis, and Athena transform the way you view your life, make room for the triple goddess. For she has a lot to show you!

## Sage Goddess

I listen to the sage crone because she is the ultimate goddess: bold, brassy, and sharp. Each sage goddess remembers her past, learns from mistakes, and imparts that wisdom upon her seekers. Her character may come across as harsh, but it is because she is introspective, intuitive, and often reflecting on the past, yet ready to embark on the future. Her work is nitty-gritty and dirty. She binds problems, dissolves blocks, and banishes weaknesses. The sage goddess is deep, proud, and knowledgeable. In one word, the sage goddess energies are all about regeneration.

### Sage Goddess: Rhea's Story

After the creation of the universe, the Titans were the first to rule. These elder gods roamed the universe for an untold amount of time. Rhea was the Titaness queen. Like her mother, Gaea (Earth), she claimed the title of supreme goddess of fertility. Even Rhea's name translated to the words "flow" and "ease" in reference to menstruation and childbirth.

When the great goddess became pregnant with her children, the father, Cronus, was haunted by an omen that if fully grown, one of his sons would overthrow him and take over his position as leader. Out of jealousy and fear, Cronus swallowed all five of his children when they were born: Demeter, Hades, Hera, Hestia, and Poseidon. When Rhea became pregnant for the sixth time, she fled to the mountains of Crete in hiding.

Cronus tracked her down and demanded the baby. Rhea's assistants distracted Cronus while the goddess placed the baby in a cave and handed Cronus a large rock wrapped in a blanket. The Titan didn't bother to inspect the whole bundle; instead, he swallowed it whole. Rhea's trick had worked, and it would eventually pay off.

Zeus was raised by Rhea's attendants, and when he was fully grown, Zeus left the mountains and went in search of his father, Cronus. Once he found his father, Zeus caused Cronus to regurgitate his siblings. The five Olympic gods united with Zeus to fight Cronus and the Titans for power.

After a long and bloody battle, the Titans fell out of power and Zeus became supreme leader. Rhea then disputed with her son Zeus over her privileges. She demanded to be given her due portion of heaven, sea, and earth. After all, she was the one who spared his life and hid him from his father.

Zeus ultimately refused her request and, in anger, the goddess retreated to the mountains, accompanied by her attendants, and surrounded herself with wild creatures.

## Ancient Worship of Rhea

Rhea was worshiped as the "Mother of the Gods," "The Great Mountain Mother," "Mother of Wild Creatures," and simply, "Mother Earth."

Rhea's Greek background places her art in Crete, which is also where her followers held rituals in her name. They celebrated by clashing cymbals and kettles, and beating drums. Specific ceremonies of wild dancing and mystical procreation rites were said to reveal her powers.

Among her many symbols are the blazing torch, the chariot drawn by lions, and the double ax. Her colors are dark earth tones: deep green, charcoal gray, black, and brown.

## Your Sage Goddess

In Rhea's story, she fights for her children and uses her quick wit to outsmart Cronus. She battles with the men in her life, first Cronus and then Zeus. Rhea eventually retires to the mountains. I don't blame her for not wanting to stick around!

It was her passion and perseverance that made the Titan goddess keep pushing forward. In the end she survived. Rhea is an inspiration to us all. Wisdom comes through years of living but also through trials and tribulations. Each fight, each day is a test of character. The sage goddess Rhea is a counselor.

Using the colors and associations above, construct a ritual in her name if you'd like to connect with her energies. Or call upon her name when you wish to be shown the right path.

## Sister Goddess

I listen to the sister goddess because she is smart, strong, and driven. Every sister goddess craves to explore, move, and create, for she is energy and fluid movement. Youth and beauty don't overshadow her intellect or her heroic characteristics. In one word, the sister goddess is hope.

Persephone, a Greek goddess, illustrates these traits perfectly. In some societies she was referred to as Kore, which translates to "maiden." Her story is that of courage and endurance.

## Nurturing Goddess

I listen to the nurturing goddess because she protects, loves, and cares. Every nurturing goddess illuminates with generosity in her presence—she makes an effort so no one feels empty, unfulfilled, or brokenhearted.

It is through her fertility that the nurturing goddess takes the reins of life. She embodies powerful character traits: the ability to listen, forgive, and understand. The nurturing goddess is the universal key shown in each and every culture. In one word, the nurturing goddess is healing.

Demeter, a Greek goddess, conveys these same characteristics with her story of maternal love, grief, sadness, and loss.

### The Sister and Nurturing Goddesses:
### Persephone and Demeter's Story

Persephone, the sister goddess in this story, was a youthful maiden and daughter of the earth goddess, Demeter. The story begins with Hades, the king of the Underworld, and how he was entranced by Persephone's beauty. He instantly fell in love with her and thought her radiance would brighten the land of the shadowy dead.

Hades put in a request to Zeus that he would like to take the maiden as his wife, and Zeus agreed. So, one day when Persephone wandered to pick narcissus flowers, the earth shook and the Underworld revealed a black horse-drawn chariot.

In the blink of an eye, Hades took Persephone by her wrist and abducted the young maiden, taking her back down to the depths of the Underworld. Demeter heard her daughter's cry and wandered the earth in search of her child. As the mother searched, she neglected the green earth and with each passing day a cold frost came upon the land. Demeter refused to return to Mount Olympus after hearing from Helios (the sun god) that Zeus let Hades take her daughter without her consent. Instead of living with the other gods, she roamed among the mortals, disguising herself as a human.

One day in Eleusis, Demeter, wearing her blue-green cloak, sat by a well and was approached by four concerned maidens. They felt pity for the sad woman and ran back home to ask their mother if they could take her in. Metaneira, their mother, agreed and took the woman into their home. However, Demeter didn't stay with them long because she was discovered in an attempt to make

Metaneira's son, Demophoon, a god. Demeter revealed her true identity as a radiant goddess and instructed Metaneira to build a temple in her name.

Once the temple was completed, Demeter sat there alone, wilting away with longing for her daughter. That year without Persephone made Demeter withhold her gifts from the earth, creating terrible drought and famine. Zeus finally intervened and sent Hermes, the messenger god, to the Underworld. He was instructed to fetch Hades's bride and return the maiden to her mother.

Unhappy with her abduction and surroundings, Persephone was eager to leave the desolate place and return to her familiar environment. At Hermes's word, Persephone knew she'd be reunited with Demeter, as his demand was the direct order of Zeus.

Reluctant to see his love go, upon saying good-bye Hades made Persephone eat a pomegranate seed. He knew once she'd eaten food in the land of the dead Persephone would always be connected to his realm.

Finally, Persephone was united with her mother, Demeter, and the earth mother heard the news of the pomegranate seed. Demeter feared she'd lose her daughter forever, but Rhea, Zeus's mother, came quickly with a message.

In compromise, the other gods declared that one-third (four months) of the year, Persephone would go to the Underworld and reside in the kingdom of darkness. Thus, Demeter's sadness during that time created harsh and barren fields—fall and winter. However, Demeter, as the earth mother, would also rejuvenate the land and make the fields rich again for the spring and summer when Persephone was not down in the depths of the Underworld.

## Ancient Worship of Persephone and Demeter

Persephone was honored as "Goddess of the Underworld, or Death," as well as "Maiden of Spring and Summer." Her symbols are the narcissus flower and the pomegranate seed. Persephone's colors are youthful pink and passionate red. Her myth conveys the story of life, death, and rebirth, which are celebrated in specific rituals called the Eleusinian Mysteries.

Persephone's mother, Demeter, had several names: "Goddess of the Corn, Harvest Wealth, Vegetation, and Fertility." Her offerings were supposed to remain in their natural state: uncooked grain, unspun wool, or fresh fruits. Demeter's colors are earthy greens, brown, and orange. Her symbols are cornflowers, grains, wheat, and a blue-green cloak.

She taught mankind the art of farming so they no longer had to live as nomads, roaming the earth. Along with Persephone, her story was played out in the sacred Eleusinian Mysteries. The earth mother, Demeter, was also honored yearly in April for the Thesmophoria Festival.

## Your Sister Goddess

Persephone is torn between her mother and her love interest, Hades. The young goddess has to negotiate her time because she's often pulled at from all angles. Many teens can relate to this feeling. Persephone adapts, changes, and creates her own happiness. When you seek her strength and power, look within. Or use the above color symbols and associations to create a ritual in her name. Light candles, find flowers, and ask for your sister goddess to come to your aid in a time of need.

## Your Nurturing Goddess

In her story, Demeter obsessed to the point of putting the earth in danger. This shows her supreme devotion to and love for her daughter. She is one of the only Greek goddesses who knew pain.

Through our teenage years, some young women feel lost, abandoned, or unloved. They are painful emotions but they can be subdued. Just as the earth mother, Demeter, called for her child, the nurturing goddess calls for you. She is always by your side, full of help and love, and she sends you her renewing positive energies.

When you seek comfort and protection, call upon Demeter. Create a ritual in her name to connect with the nurturing goddess energies. She is divine and all encompassing. Her door is always open.

## ✳ Revival of the Goddess

Imagine the ancient Greeks holding long festivals in the summer, dancing nude by bonfires, living with the farm animals, and offering sacrifices to the gods in appreciation of the harvest. That is certainly a unique approach to camping! Sometimes in our contemporary visions we see the ancient people and their cultures as strange, uncivilized, or barbaric.

They lived off the land, and it was their world. Almost everything was sowed and reaped by hand. So one could image a big celebration once the harvest came, because their work had paid off. And they would not forget how the earth mother blessed them with their bounty. This is why farming and the gods were linked. Even today, contemporary goddess cultures find reference to festivals and celebrations for the harvest times.

True, the ancient people also had enough spare time to call upon Aphrodite for a little nudge in the love department or Apollo for some musical guidance. Yet in the end, there is no question about the role deities played in the ancient Greeks' lives. The great Olympic gods all had their own interesting stories because the people wanted that identification with divine. It is easier for humans to accept death if they are told they will be greeted by Persephone, the beautiful maiden goddess, when they reach the other side.

Through belief in their gods, the ancient people developed a sense of wholeness and strength. This is the thread that links each culture and religion. People want something to believe in; we all crave spiritual empowerment. This is why divinity is universal. Aside from the ancient Greeks, other ancient cultures honored deities and passed down the stories through each generation. The Egyptian, Native American, Chinese, Japanese, Celtic, and Norse people each honored their own set of gods. These pantheons are just a handful of the cultures waiting to be explored.

You may want to read up on your particular background. Whether you have Italian, Slavic, African, or Indian ancestors, there are stories and myths out there craving to be consumed and rejuvenated. The goddesses need not remain dormant anymore. Uncover a story and discover yourself. This is a step in the revival of the goddess.

JOURNAL EXERCISE—*Once you find a goddess you identify with, research her qualities, symbols, and associations to develop a prayer in her name (see the Aphrodite, Artemis, and Athena sections in this chapter as examples). Your personal invocation can be spoken or chanted when you would like to call upon your particular goddess's energies.*

## GODDESS WITHIN RITUAL

The purpose of this ritual is more than acknowledging your inner goddess. It is a ritual that invites her out!

**SUPPLIES:**

a white votive

one teaspoon olive oil

matches (or lighter)

bowl of dirt (earth)

Find a quiet place to work where you won't be disturbed. Gather all your supplies in front of you. Preferably you'll want a hard surface to work on, like a desk or table. You'll be working with a candle, so be careful if lighting matches. Move dangling fabrics out of the way beforehand and clear the surface of anything flammable.

The first step is blessing the candle. You do this by holding the bottom with one hand and rubbing olive oil on it in a clockwise motion with the other. Visualize a positive ball of energy surrounding the candle with light.

Next, hold the candle above the bowl of earth and sprinkle a bit of dirt lightly over the candle while saying this chant:

> **Earth arms stretched**
> **Oneness, divine**
> **Mother nature, fullness, power growing, energy**
> **Please bless this candle for positive use!**

Then make a hole in the pile of dirt with your fingers. This hole should be large in width and rather deep. When the earthen hole is the

right size, drop your candle in. Carefully light the wick and proceed to
say the following out loud or mentally to yourself:

Goddess within emerge in light
Come to the surface, beam with glory
Treasured mystical
Goddess I look your way
I call from within
I ask for your knowingness
I seek your guidance
I hear, listen, contemplate
Message of hope
Path of courage
Light in the darkness
I become enchantress
Fearless
Powerful
Me.

Open this book to the next journal page and write down all the
qualities you imagine your inner goddess might have: strong will,
faith, understanding, compassion, and so forth. Reflect on the ritual.
When you feel the time is right, blow out the candle and go about the
rest of your day.

You can relight the candle or perform the ritual again anytime you
feel the need to get in touch with your inner goddess.

JOURNAL EXERCISE—*In conjunction with the goddess ritual, use this space to list qualities of your inner goddess.*

_____

_____

_____

_____

_____

_____

_____

_____

_____

_____

_____

_____

_____

_____

_____

_____

_____

_____

_____

_____

_____

_____

# CHAPTER FOUR

# Heal and forgive

## Life Issues

L IFE ISN'T ALWAYS filled with smiles or happy memories. In this chapter, we will address the other side of the soul—the darkness within, pain deep down inside—and try to find some sort of closure. Closure isn't forgetting or denying the pain and past issue, it's giving yourself permission to put the past in the past and move on.

Aching pain on your soul can be draining. In chapter one, I talked about teens being "blocked." Holding on to the past can also create a block and prevent you from living the life you deserve. Everyone, rich or poor, tall or short, has had issues in their life. I remember watching TV one day and an actress was talking about her deceased husband. Even though he had passed on a good several years before, when the woman talked about it, you could still see the hurt and pain in her eyes. It may seem to a casual observer that the actress was simply overreacting or holding on to the past, but that death had a serious impact on her life and inner spirit. The woman's love for her husband was so profound that his death seemed fresh, as if it had occurred the week before the interview.

If something is weighing you down, no matter how big or small, then it's having a profound and intense impact on your soul. It may seem silly to someone else, but your "issues" matter. They matter because everything that goes on in your life shapes who you are, and hey, let's face it, you are highly important—you matter.

I could make a small list of events and comments that still on occasion weigh me down; one memory still sticks out in my mind. One time in junior high I was waiting in line in the cafeteria and struck up a conversation with this guy I barely knew. That was a big deal for me because in junior high I was in that awkward stage where talking with males my age was totally uncomfortable.

At the end of the conversation he said to me, "You're a nice person." My heart jumped because I thought that meant he liked me, but then he continued, "You could be cool if you dressed better and lost some weight." I was crushed, but my best friend came to my rescue and gave him a piece of her mind!

That was years ago, and yet I still remember his exact words and how much, in that moment, they stung. I finally chose not to let comments like that affect my whole life. I affirm myself; people like that aren't worth my energy! Now I scoff at that unpleasant incident because that kid knew nothing about me, who I was, and the impact I would have on people in the future with my writing. After a five-minute conversation he decided what was best for me and the way I live? Now that's downright rude!

Words hurt. Even a couple of passive comments can stick with you for years. You can't take them out of your life with a pretty pink eraser. They are imprinted on the past, one moment in time.

In the end, it's how you deal with these issues that matter! You can give in and let other people's words rule your life, or you can take back the power.

The soul is a complex thing easily pleased and easily hurt, especially if you happen to be a teenager. People our age are still growing, learning, and evolving. How can a person overcome issues? Is there any way to deal with the pain? What steps should a person take to banish the darkness and start fresh?

That is exactly what this chapter is for—to answer those questions. Don't worry, you'll have me by your side, blank journal pages for expression, and a ritual of closure to help initiate a fresh start and move on!

##  Acknowledge the Pain

I refuse to believe any one person's life is perfect. True, some people appear as if they "have it all," but that doesn't mean they are devoid of fear and sadness. Part of the human condition are the emotional ups and downs and the good days and bad days. Deep pain and hurt also belong within this category.

Being a teenager is a full-time job. We are emotionally in tune because we have the ability to closely remember the feelings of childhood and get a good taste of the adult world. I hate it when people blame our emotions and expressions on "hormones." They act as if those teen hormones are demons taking over their innocent children. Granted, things are changing inside and all around us, but it is because of these changes that we, the "hormone-driven teens," adapt, accept, and come into ourselves as adults.

We are automatically adjusting our gears, and that requires us to pay attention to our emotional and intuitive happenings. And yet, through all these changes, it is so easy to push aside past pain. It's as if there isn't enough time in the day between school, homework, family, and friends, and the pain gets stashed away to be dealt with later.

If you're nodding your head in agreement, then it's about time you changed your methods. Pushing issues aside is not healthy, and inevitably you're bound to a self-destructive pattern. Acknowledge your hurt, pain, and despair. Use your energy to heal yourself, instead of using it to hide from your problems.

JOURNAL EXERCISE—*Write a letter to your soul. Make a solemn promise that you won't let your past disrupt your future. Right in this moment, free your inhibitions and hesitations. Tell your soul that you're ready to tackle the issues in your life, past and present.*

# ✳ Life Issues

I see life through the eyes of a teenager. I know the adversity teen women can go through. Unfair teachers, bullies, low self-esteem, hurtful siblings, neglective parents. Life at times seems cold, harsh, and lonely. You crave the youthful summers of your childhood and think back to a time when playing house with a best friend made the day feel complete. Then there are deeper pains and stronger negative situations: drugs, pressures to have sex, or an abusive person controlling your life.

Teenagers can be raped by strangers, abused by family members, and emotionally wrecked by young men who claim to love them. If you're different than everyone else, your uniqueness can at times be seen as a sickness. A different family situation, appearance, or sexual preference—things you can't, won't, and don't control—can lead to discrimination and loneliness.

Every teenager has issues and heartbreak. We've all suffered in one way or another. The internal demons can drive us to the point of obsession. Am I thin enough? How could I live if he left me? They are right, I am ugly. It's my fault, I deserve to be hit and punished. These are the thoughts of the girl down the street. The brunette you sit behind in English class and the teen five lockers down. Have you identified with any of the comments above? If you let your issues take over your life, you'll sound like them too.

I don't know what pain has been caused, how you've suffered, or what hurdles you face every day. I do know that being out of balance and out of control is not healthy for your mind, body, or soul.

In the grand scheme of things, it is more likely that you're facing issues of less intensity than rape or abuse. Yet as I mentioned before, your experiences are yours alone and can't be judged on a scale of "lesser" or "greater" than another's experience. Just because you are dealing with a bully and another woman your age is working through a rape trauma doesn't mean your issue is any less important. There is no scale of judgment when evil shadows have touched your life.

The past has been tugging on you long enough; you are not a lost cause. You have your inner goddess, people around you who care, and you also have me, to help guide you out of the darkness, into the light. Let's work together to tackle the issues in your life, past and present.

JOURNAL EXERCISE—*Map out issues that you have bottled up inside. Explain in detail the matter at hand, when it happened, and what emotional tolls it has taken.*

_____

_____

_____

_____

_____

_____

_____

_____

_____

_____

_____

_____

# ✳ Dealing with Death

As teenagers, it seems on the outside as if we are independent and don't need our families. Yet when a death occurs, it does provide a wake-up call. The message can be heard loud and clear. We always need our loved ones in one way or another.

The title of this section is Dealing with Death, but in reality there is no true way to "deal" with the death of a loved one. You make strong efforts to get out of bed and start each day even when that simple step seems like a struggle.

My most profound experiences with death have been from my two dogs dying. I'll admit the passing of a person and death of a pet are two distinct things, but it's not to say that the same pain and anguish won't result. A death in the family is one of the hardest things to go through, no matter if it is a person or pet. Some say real love doesn't discriminate—well, neither does death.

I honestly cannot fathom what it's like when a parent dies. I haven't experienced that pain or emotion. But I know someone who has. My best friend, Seetal, lost her biological father when she was rather young. Her mother remarried, but the pain of losing a parent never seemed to have left. I could sense this because her voice would change slightly when she mentioned him. Sadness has a way of striking in an instant.

I was hesitant to write about this subject because I am not an expert on death, but then again, who is? I have been lucky in the sense that I haven't encountered much death in my family. But you only need to go through that experience once to be all-encompassed by the feeling of sadness. With any deeply life-altering event, the best thing to do is express your feelings and emotions. Talking about the issue helps, but if you're not the type to voice your pain, try writing about it. Journal writing, poetry, even art can release your emotions without having to say a word out loud. Pain is private and if you feel it's best, meditate and pray on your own.

The whole point of expressing yourself or "dealing with death" is to address your pain, fear, and anger head-on. It's okay to be angry when someone dies. Just remember to channel the anger in a way so you don't hurt anyone, including yourself.

Once a death has occurred in your life, you will never be the same person again. By experiencing death, family and friends assess the way they live. Hopefully, you'll change your ways for the better and focus on important life issues that you've been ignoring.

JOURNAL EXERCISE—*If someone you love has passed away whom you would like to honor, place his or her picture where you'll see it often. Light a candle while drawing on your positive memories together. Do something sincere and memorable in his or her name.*

*In the space provided, take the time to write a loving note. This is your chance to apologize, express your gratitude, and tell that person how much you still care.*

# ✳ Healing

It is through living that we encounter blessed events and find new things to be grateful for. Each day brings some piece of fruitful knowledge or an intense, unforgettable memory. Unfortunately, some of these memories and events are not positive. In fact, they are so negative that some memories can leave a dark spot on your soul, within your life, and etched in your mind. What can you do about this now? Well, you have two choices: Leave things the way they are or fight for the happiness you want.

Your experiences are yours alone. No one else has ever walked in your shoes, seen through your eyes, or felt your pain. You have a right to be upset over your past and the negative things you've encountered. Eventually you'll need to stop dwelling on the past, because if you don't, you will miss out on the beauty of the present moment. Or worse, forget the excitement of the future and its amazing possibilities.

You can overcome your issues, but to do so you have to make the conscious decision—allow yourself to move on. If you let those pain-filled memories continuously rule your life, they will suffocate your happiness.

Make the choice at this moment in time to put the past away and let yourself heal. By healing you won't be giving up your ability to feel pain from your issues, nor are you letting someone else win. You are taking back your passion for life and growing as an individual.

# ✳ Closure

The process of healing from a traumatic event, memory, or death might take months or years—there is no time line to compete with.

I never agreed with the saying "Time heals all wounds." Time dulls the memory and stifles the pain to some degree, but for some things in life the wound never dissipates completely. A lot of teens blame themselves for past issues. This isn't a healthy way to live. There is a difference between taking responsibility for one's actions and coming down on yourself for every negative event that has occurred in your life within the past five years.

Learn to forgive yourself.

Forgive yourself for the mistakes you've made.

Forgive yourself for not knowing the full truth or what's best.

Forgiving yourself for getting into tricky situations and making a mess of your life.

Forgive yourself, because if you do not, you won't ever find the closure you so desperately seek.

There isn't much you can do about the past. Some issues can be rectified, like apologizing to an ex-boyfriend for ending a relationship in such a harsh manner. Positive friendships can arise after a few months of cooling down. If you aren't sorry, then don't apologize. Apologies are best said when they are from the heart and sincere. Especially keep your distance from young men who have hurt you physically or emotionally.

For current issues plaguing your life, you can take back control. Speak out and get help. I had a bully harassing me and thought the problem would blow over eventually. Instead, the problem got much worse. There came a point where I couldn't stand it any longer. I stuck up for myself by telling the proper people and getting her off my back.

From that experience, I truly came to realize how important expressing your problems and seeking help can be. Communicate your feelings and get help if you feel someone in your life is hurting you. There are organizations, teachers, guidance counselors, and friends who will stand with you. It is all out there for the taking; you just need to ask for the help. Remember, you are not alone in this world and you don't have to go through this process by yourself.

In conclusion, healing, forgiving, and tackling your issues can bring closure. It might take a while, but you will be able to move on. Follow your heart, trust your instincts, and trust me when I say you'll eventually find the peace you deserve.

## BURY THE DARKNESS –
## A RITUAL OF HEALING

*Perform this ritual when you are ready to put the past in its place and change your life for the better.*

**SUPPLIES:**

a sunny afternoon

a sheet (blanket or towel) to put on the ground outside

a pen

a blank piece of paper

a handheld gardening shovel (or large spoon)

a bowl filled with water

a memory token (picture or piece of jewelry that gives you comfort or pleasant memories)

one teaspoon of basil

one teaspoon of salt

a paper towel to dry your hands

On a sunny afternoon gather all your supplies, dress accordingly, and head outside. Don't forget to bring this book with you! Find a quiet spot to set up, preferably someplace where you can bury something small. Lay down your blanket and calm yourself with a few deep breaths. Take in the warm atmosphere. Remember that mother nature is self-healing and all through this ritual she is with you, right underneath you.

To begin the ritual of healing, take your pen and paper and write about issues and negative experiences that haunt you. Don't go into detail here, just provide a brief overview. Fold the piece of paper up to a small square and put it aside for a few moments. Visually locate an out-of-the-way place where you can bury the paper. Make sure nobody will dig or garden in that area. Right under an old tree or bush is perfect.

Go to your selected spot and dig a deep hole. It doesn't have to be wide, just deep enough to drop the paper in and completely cover it. Once you've dug your hole, drop the squared paper in and push the dirt back on top. After it's buried, place one hand over the dirt pile and say this chant out loud or to yourself:

> Mother earth, rock, mineral, dirt, and salt.
> Take my pain, humility, anger, and anguish
> Nourish my life, wrap me in your loving arms.

Turn away from the pile and walk back to your tools and blanket. Know that your past has been buried and sent into mother earth to be absorbed and disintegrated. If you're feeling upset, hold your memory token in your hands and visualize a white light of positive energy around you. Remember that you are in control of the present moment.

The next step is to cleanse the energies within your soul. Place the bowl of water in front of you and throw in the salt and basil. If it's more convenient, the basil and salt may be mixed before you go outside.

Stir softly with your index finger and submerge both of your hands into the bowl.

Say this chant out loud or mentally:

*I bathe in the rays of light,*
*That shine ever so bright,*
*I cleanse my mind of all things bad and bane,*
*Let my life be void of pain.*

Visualize the pure energies of water streaming up your arms into your whole body. Take your hands out and dry them with the paper towel.

The last step is completely about visualization. You're going to create a protection sphere to block out future negative energies.

Close your eyes and erect a bright white mist around your body. Let it turn into a green color, as green represents earth. Your connection to the earth is through this imagery. If you have a hard time visualizing, try to bring up the feeling of being safe and protected. Hold the visualization for as long as you can. This is your protection shield. You have the right to erect it at any time your feel it is necessary.

Once you feel your shield has enveloped you in protection, let the visualization fade. Stay seated for a few moments to regain your full awareness of the surroundings. After deep visualizing, it often feels as if you've just woken from a soft dream state, so it's best to move slowly at first.

The ritual is complete. If you'd like, say a small prayer of thanks to your deity or mother earth for her positive energies and assistance. Empty the water on the ground and carry your other tools back inside. Relax, take time for yourself, or write in the journal space provided detailing your ritual experiences.

# CHAPTER FIVE

# Catch a Shooting Star

## Wishes, Hopes, and Dreams

D O YOU REMEMBER when you were a child and someone would ask you, "What do you want to be when
you grow up?" There wasn't a feeling of restrictions;
everything seemed possible. Over time that feeling fades away and
the real world sinks in. You grow into the realization that there
are limits to every dream. Maybe your family has set expectations.
Parents have a tendency to influence goals or push their children
into "the family business."

When was the last time someone asked you what you wanted
out of life? What about your hopes and dreams? I am not just talking about college and careers, I am talking about true desires and
happiness.

There are times when you have an idea of what you're looking
for, but nothing seems to "click" together. Well, you're a teenager
and you've now reached a crossroads in your life. Some paths lead

to happiness, others lead to disappointment. If only there were clear signs on where to travel!

There is no surefire way to getting ultimate happiness, but who ever said it isn't worth a try! In this chapter we're going to work together, in conjunction with some journal exercises, to figure all of this madness out and find some clarity for the road ahead. The first step? Finding your passion!

## ✳ finding Your Passion

Finding your passion isn't about sexuality, it is about your dreams and aspirations for life. Passion is embedded desire, a deep, mysterious yearning. It's time to latch on to those powerful emotions and truly embrace the things you crave to do!

Let's move slightly off topic. Picture yourself a week from now, happy and fulfilled. What are you doing in that visualization? Singing, dancing, playing your favorite sport, or just hanging out with a group of friends? Happiness isn't always defined by winning a trophy or getting the lead part in the school play. Those are accomplishments, which are great, but being happy in the process—feeling alive—is what makes those experiences worthwhile.

Now let's get back on topic and think about the future! What would you like to be doing in ten years? What would make you happy and content? Try not to think of the actual accomplishment but the path of actions and process you'd go through.

Want to be a singer? Then you'll have to work hard to train your voice and then get your name out in the business. Fame isn't automatic or guaranteed. Would you still love to sing even if your ultimate dream doesn't come true?

If the answer is yes, then you've defined one of your passions. Hey, who made the rule that says you can only have one passionate dream? It's up to you to decided how many you want to conjure up!

JOURNAL EXERCISE—*Write down all the things you're passionate about—your wildest dreams and future aspirations.*

# ✳ Define Your Goals

Listening to your heart and finding your passion is a rare thing. Most people don't like to imagine the possibilities because they'd rather not consider a negative outcome. This is where your cynical mind kicks in and boots out that "silly dream." What about a compromise? Isn't it possible to incorporate one of your passions into your future, all the while actually accomplishing something? Of course it's possible; the key is to think realistically and define your goals!

When people plan to travel, they lay out the map and plot the best way to get from one place to another. That's exactly why defining your goals is so important, because once you have a destination, the next step is developing the best plan to actually get yourself there.

This is also why having realistic goals is important. Add your heart's passion with reality and give it a mix! What did you come out with? Maybe your passion for dancing turns into a goal of teaching young kids how to tap dance. Or the dream of being the first female president develops into you becoming president of a big organization that helps woman and children in need. Realistic goals bring realistic results. However, don't shy away from your heart's passion. There are many ways of accomplishing your desires and finding happiness at the same time.

JOURNAL EXERCISE—*Now that you have an idea of what your passions are, try creating a small list of realistic goals.*

## ✳ Following the Goal

It seems somewhat easy to set a goal; the tricky part is actually walking the path to achieve it! This is why you start out slow with small baby steps. Many corporate offices offer internships. Some colleges will let you join "job-study programs." So, if your goal is to be in the news business, a local news station might let you work behind the scenes. You would actually be working in the newscasting environment and learning hands-on what it takes to be a technician, video journalist, sports writer, and so forth.

The majority of these programs will put you to work, but they won't pay you a salary. However, the experience would look great on a resume. Being active in pursuit of your goal is great and self-empowering, but don't stress yourself out. Serious goals take time to accomplish. If you're too young to be hired as an intern, then read up about the field, study as much as you can, and soak up the knowledge. You'll be glad you did because most hard work pays off in the end.

## ✳ Fighting the Fight

Sometimes it seems even with a realistic goal that your family won't support you. Or even worse, you've stopped believing in yourself and your abilities to succeed. If you aspire to do the things you love, you're going to have to fight other people's negativity and a handful of your own.

It's easy to give up but much harder to push forward toward your goals. I find that it's helpful to identify why I am fighting myself. Is it because I am doubtful of the work and time it takes? Am I fearing other people's opinions and reactions? Afraid of change? Or maybe just a bit scared that the goal I had two months ago isn't one I'd want to pursue anymore? Once I've determined why I have hesitation, I can tackle that issue individually and work out the problem. In the end, whether you sabotage your dream is your own choice.

It is equally hard when a family member or friend isn't too keen on your aspirations. Try not to let their opinions shatter your dreams, because it is your life, your decisions, and your future. You might want to avoid talking about your goal when they are around. That's a mature, responsible way of handling other people's negativity. As one female to another, trust me when I say that getting into a fight over the situation won't make matters better. Do listen to them if they are telling you your future plans might get you hurt or in trouble.

Running away to Hollywood in pursuit of an acting career isn't a "realistic goal" or a healthy one. Remember to always stay smart and empower yourself through reasonable goals. Keep focused, work hard, but most of all believe in yourself, because without faith in your abilities you'll have a much harder time achieving your ultimate desires.

JOURNAL EXERCISE—*Make a list of internal arguments that get between you and your goal. Once the list is complete, take a few minutes and ask yourself why you're letting these hesitations block your impassioned pursuit.*

# ✳ The Passion for Now

Most of this chapter concerns your future, mainly your career and your life's path. Yet sometimes people, especially teens, are so busy looking toward the future that we forget to live in the present. The small passions get pushed aside and the big goals take center stage. Having future aspirations is fantastic, but don't forget the passion for now! Love to write poetry? Don't keep pushing it out of your way, mind, or heart. Pursue all passions, even the small, everyday ones, because they'll make your quality of life that much sweeter. As silly as it sounds, partaking in comforting interests will make you less stressed.

I know exactly what it's like to have everything pile up! Often outside influences push aside the little things I love to do. Yet every day I fight for just a few minutes to myself. I like to take that time to chat with friends online, write in a journal, or create jewelry. It's great to keep busy, but also keep your dreams and passions alive by giving them the time of day.

JOURNAL EXERCISE—*Write down three small passions you enjoy doing but feel that you never have the time for.*

## RITUAL FOR DREAMS

This is a two-part ritual. First you'll banish fear and free your inhibitions. Then you'll create a wish charm to send your "wishful" intentions out into the world!

**PART ONE**

**SUPPLIES:**

a black marker

a fallen leaf

a windy day

On a nice, windy day, travel outside with the black marker and this book in hand. Find a large leaf on the ground. If you can't locate one that has fallen, approach a tree and ask for permission to take a leaf, then pull one off gently. Next, take out your pen or marker and write the words "no fear" on one side. Hold it in your hand and think about your future goals. Visualize yourself actually being where you want to be, without fear or hesitation.

Next, say the following phrase:

> I fear not for I am free,
> I pursue my goals with endurance,
> I aspire to be great,
> I reap the rewards for which I have sown,
> I fear not anymore.

Last, hold your arm out and, when the wind blows, let the leaf go. Don't follow it with your eyes, simply turn around and return inside.

Prepare for the second part of this ritual. This next half doesn't have to be performed on the same day, but preferably within the same week.

**PART TWO**

**SUPPLIES:**

a white envelope

a recent picture of you

approximately two tablespoons of sugar (in small bowl)

a dried flower of your choice

a shiny penny

This part of the ritual is best done on the night of a full moon. As expressed in chapter two, the full moon is when power is at its highest concentration. You'll want to harness these energies for the creation of your wish charm!

To start, find a quiet, private place to work, and bring your supplies with you. Take a deep breath and visualize your protective sphere of white light around your body.

Say the following incantation out loud or in your mind. When each

item is mentioned, such as the dried flower, pick that item up in your hand and send it your positive flowing energy.

Under a full moon shining bright
I seek the power of luna's light
A penny for my wish
Dried flower so it may grow
Dash of sugar for sweetened results
And one pretty photo
Desire of mine be heard
Send and seal my wish and passion
In an uncontrolling fashion
I create my dream now
So be it here in the very moment and time
Scared still with this rhyme!

Next, it's time to create the wish charm itself. Open the envelope and place your picture in first. Make sure you can see the photo as you place the penny, dried flower, and sugar inside. Before you go to seal the envelope, mentally picture your goal and see yourself happy.

Last, seal up the envelope and tuck it somewhere safe. The charm is done; pack everything up and take the night off for yourself!

## More About This Ritual

The process of letting your fears go with the wind isn't a new one. In fact, it's an old superstition. The small phrase you spoke right before letting go is an anagram. Look at the words again: free, endurance, aspire, and reap. The first letter of each of these words spells out "fear." The very thing you were working to let go.

The second part of the ritual asks you to create a charm. The picture represents you and who you are. As the rest of the poem states, the penny represents your wish, the flower calls upon the power of earth and growth, and sugar makes the desired outcome sweet! The charm will have power and aid you in reaching your goals, so long as you believe in its abilities.

CHAPTER SIX

# Angels by Your Side
## Celestial Guidance

ANGELS ARE CELESTIAL beings that live on a plane of existence parallel to ours. The very word *angel* comes from the Greek *angelos,* meaning "messenger," and the Persian *angaros,* which roughly translates to the word "courier."

No, angels aren't in charge of dropping off business packages; instead, they are said to carry the direct voice of our creator, the higher powers, whomever you believe him, her, or them to be. Angels are messengers that offer guidance, inspiration, healing energies, and companionship. Angels are real and people have believed in them so strongly for centuries. Strangers who walk past each other on the street may very well be linked through this ethereal belief. Beautiful, celestial beings touch our lives in subtle, unseen ways on a daily basis.

When working on the outline for this book, I wasn't sure if I should include a chapter on angels. My hesitation wasn't because I don't believe in them (as I strongly believe in their presence), it was because I didn't want *Moonbeams & Shooting Stars* to lean toward the religious side of things. Faith in a higher power is amazing and healthy, but the message for this book is to inspire teen women like you and me to believe in ourselves and reclaim our inner power.

Then I remembered something I had read a while back in a book called *An Angel in Your Pocket*. Rosemary Ellen Guiley, the author, stated several examples of how angels aren't only a Catholic belief, but they are universally found in almost every religion throughout the world. Now, that was amazing to learn. Angels can be for everyone, regardless of religion or path!

Most of all, angels are helping entities and companions, something I believe anyone could use in their life. Angels can be viewed without the religious undertones if you look directly into their core message and purpose. Which is coincidentally the same way we are going to delve into this chapter.

You'll also find information in regard to angels and how they have been viewed throughout history, art, and various cultures. In addition to that, material on guardian angels will surely capture your interest. Finally, to finish up the chapter, you'll find a cute and touching ritual that's bound to open your eyes to the angelic powers surrounding you and your life.

## ✳ The Angelic Touch

It's hard to write this section on angels without filtering in my personal beliefs or feelings. I see this as a good thing because my view of these celestial beings isn't complex or too deep to explain. I've always had the feeling that they are real. Nobody drilled it into my head or told me what I must believe. I came to the conclusion on my own, after I looked deep within myself and questioned their existence. The answer I came up with after this internal search was rather simple: Yes, they do exist. I'll trust my intuition on this one. And hey, if what the experts say is true, that angels have a special connection with the human soul, then maybe it was an angel sitting on my shoulder or whispering in my ear that led me to this conclusion.

Some people are fortunate enough to have had an angel touch their lives. I believe that I am one of them. Don't worry, I am not going into a story about seeing an angel in my bedroom, with big wings, a halo, and carrying a message from God. My experience was as subtle and soft as two tugs on a shirt—literally.

Years ago on my brother's birthday, I was standing in the kitchen by our table. It was a fairly long kitchen with wooden floors and high white walls. The table was about eight feet away from the sink. This piece of information is important to the story, so follow with me for a few moments. My aunt was doing the dishes and my cousin, who was a toddler at the time, was wandering about. Suddenly, I felt two firm tugs on the back of my shirt. At first, I thought it was my cousin and told her to stop. My aunt said something to the effect of my cousin not being able to do anything because she was by her side the last couple of minutes.

I turned back, and my eyes confirmed it; she couldn't have tugged my shirt and run back to the sink without making any noise. Toddlers don't really run, they wobble, and the old wooden floor would have squeaked. Even today, I find this occurrence a bit of a mystery. Some might say it could have been the wind. Since when does the wind sneak up and tug on a person's shirt? Or maybe my inkling is correct, and it really was an angel making its presence known.

JOURNAL EXERCISE—*Have you ever had a mysterious encounter? Something curious or unusual that you could never fully explain?*

# ✳ The Purpose and Meaning of Angels

I believe people put too much focus on the names of angels, their hierarchy, and/or which categories they fit into. What's pushed aside among those debates is the very purpose and meaning of the angels themselves. Why do they exist? What are their roles? Do they only come for special people or dire circumstances?

Let's work backward on answering these questions. They aren't relegated to special "angel mediums" or priests; angels can come to anyone on any given occasion. Many times people turn to angels when a death or tragedy occurs because that's when we draw on their energies and assistance most. The roles of an angel are many. Some say special angels have certain domains: some watch over children, another oversees animals, several delegate between peace and issues of war.

They are divine protectors, harmonious companions who come from a family of beings unseen and unheard. They are nature spirits, spirit guides, and mystical beings who defend when necessary and aid when called upon. They are sacred.

These celestial beings exist because we need them within our lives, and we always have. Humans draw on their powers on a daily basis. Which makes the fact that angels are synonymously associated with "miracles" all the more reasonable. Miracles are unique occurrences that defy nature or science but bring about lifesaving change. People who believe they have been touched by an angelic miracle don't quite remain the same as they were before. Angels and their many messages (and miracles) are that of inspiration and perseverance.

It is a common belief that our divine messengers have supernatural intuitions. They also use their special "angel sense" to feel what we humans feel. Empathy in its purest form. That is why we relate to them on such a deep level. They embody some of the very emotions we carry. Angels understand human love, happiness, pain, and suffering. And that very unique understanding of how we work makes an angel's mission easier to accomplish.

On top of all the duties of protecting, aiding, and sprinkling of miracles, angels have one more deep task at hand. In some paths, they are known as guardians of the dead because they are said to guide souls to the other side. Whether the souls go to heaven or are reincarnated is an age-old debate, but the celestials are the ones that get them there! It's a very common belief that angels reside in between heaven and earth, traveling between the two worlds with their wings. In a sense, angels are the gatekeepers between our world and the next.

## ✳ The Image of an Angel

Angelology is the study of angels. Historians, philosophers, and great thinkers alike gather old texts (mostly religious) and cite specific references to angels and the celestial world. It's a serious undertaking, but with all the sources and all the encounters no group of people has ever been able to unequivocally agree on one little detail: What exactly does an angel look like? What is even more interesting is that some argue that angels can't even been seen at all!

There are, however, images from art and literary descriptions, as well as societies' varied perceptions. We use these archetypes as our foundation for angels' appearance traits. Some appear as children (cherubs especially take on this form), while others are fully grown adult figures, sometimes male, sometimes female. On occasion angels are said to be androgynous, meaning they have male and female characteristics within the same being.

Celestials are commonly portrayed with luminescent wings, which symbolize flight or enveloping protection. The winged Eros, an ancient Greek god of love, and Hermes, the Greek messenger god who had wing-tipped shoes, may have contributed to angels taking on the winged trait. Many cultures borrowed from the Greeks' philosophy and ideas.

Renaissance artists often painted angels with halos. The halo (also called a nimbus) symbolizes perfection and holiness. For this same reason saints are also depicted with halos. Not as common but still noteworthy is armor. Angels have been painted or described on several occasions wearing armor, which represents strength and power.

Over the course of time, the images of angels have changed. This is why there are many different versions of angel attire, gender, and height. They change because our human minds evolve, and the more complex our lives are the more complex angel personifications become. We mold their image from our own varying perceptions. From person to person, generation to generation, that perception changes. And so in the end we are left with a myriad of images to show exactly what an angel might look like.

More important than any of the appearance concerns is the acceptance of the angelic force. Once you believe in them, it matters less and less what they wear or how they appear. Awareness and becoming receptive to angel energy is a step in the right direction. From there the very meaning of angels is revived.

# ✳ Guardian Angels

Angels, at times, come across as distant and unreachable. We tend to think if an angel is out preventing famine, why would he or she help me with my problem? That's where a specific type of angel steps in, the guardian angel! This particular angel's appeal is broad ranged. The idea that each one of us is being guided through life via angelic assistance is a comforting notion.

The concept of guardian angels taps into our longing for companionship. Nobody likes to feel alone or unaided. We want guidance, especially during times of trials and tribulations. When the harsh winds of life come calling, our souls ache for shelter. A pair of angel wings might do the trick.

In general, one or more guardian angels are linked to an individual. And that angel (or group of angels) follows the human through each lifetime, or incarnation, and at every moment of every day.

Then this thought clicks in your head: So someone's watching me? More like watching over you. Angels aren't human and I doubt they care about material possessions, what you do in the bathroom, or why every night you brush your hair with exactly fifty-two strokes. Your guardian angel does care about your safety as well as important pending decisions, future aspirations, impact on society, and overall life choices.

Many angel believers have suggested that each time you acknowledge and accept your guardian's existence the more inclined they are to help. Although plenty of people who choose not to believe in angels receive a few celestial moments of guidance anyway! I guess that above statement is less of a rule and more of a suggestion. Angels will help anyone, even those who choose to believe they don't exist.

Many guardian angels have a soft presence, unseen by the naked eye, unheard by human ears. Even still, the celestial being is existing, following, shadowing your every movement off in the distance. May that bring you understanding, comfort, and peace.

If you choose to believe in angels, you don't have to conceptualize them as seven feet tall, perfect, complete with crisp white wings and toga sandals. Perceive them as you wish, using your heart, not what some "angel expert" says they are supposed to look like.

If you're looking to take your belief one step further, there is a ritual at the end of this chapter that will help you mold your energy with that of your guardian angel's. Of course, both your energies are already in sync, but acknowledging this connection and playing it out with an action makes the reality more true. Thus, it creates a sharper connection. That ritual is a starting point. From there your guardian angel is accessible to you at any moment, at any time. Call upon him or her with a poem or prayer. Even one sentence spoken aloud can help: "Angel of mine, I am in need of some guidance."

If you're in school and can't voice that phrase, remember that power comes from the written word. Write it on top of your math notes when studying, or put it on a scrap of paper and carry it with you in the back of your pocket (or in your shoe) for a test.

At night, before you go to sleep, you might want to thank your angel for his or her help and protection throughout the day. Here is something I've created:

*Guardian being*

*Protector of mine*

*Caring celestial*
*Thank you for your guidance*
*Good night.*

In conclusion, guardian angels exist to shine a light of hope into our souls, get us through a bad day, and make life a bit easier. Your belief in guardian angels is sacred and can be kept internally, treasured alone, or shared with close friends and family. It may be interesting to hear what they have to say about the subject. Angels, especially guardian angels, make unique conversation topics! Next time the thought crosses your mind, open up, talk about it, and welcome the warmth of an angel's wing.

# Religions, Cultures, and the Belief in Angels

The concept of angels can be found throughout the world. Almost all spiritual paths recognize and believe in some nonhuman form of guardian or messenger being. Even though some religions don't necessarily call the guardians/messengers "angels," their role is similar to that of angels by definition. For clarification purposes, in this chapter those unique beings who aren't directly called angels will be referred to as "angel-like."

The top three monotheistic religions, Christianity, Judaism, and Islam, all cite angels within their paths. These angels take on several roles: relaying messages, becoming guardians, and aiding God (or Allah to the Islam faith).

In the Hebrew Bible (the Old Testament), angels are identified as *malakh,* meaning messenger. Several unnamed angels came to a man named Abraham and his wife, Sarah, to inform them she was going to bear a child. Many of Abraham's descendants were visited by angels as well. These angels offered guidance, support, and comfort, but also set forth intense tests of faith. There are many angel stories found throughout Jewish scriptures. Little by little people are introduced to the cherubim, seraphim, and archangels.

Christianity expands on the Jewish idea of angels. In the New Testament, Archangel Gabriel comes to the virgin Mary to tell her she will have a child.

In the Islamic religion, the angel Djibril (the Arab name for Gabriel) is said to have helped convey the messages of the Koran from Allah to the prophet Muhammad. Other angels in Islam protect heaven's gates and glorify Allah. The Malaika, "messengers," are guardians who watch over humans and write down everything that occurs on earth. Even though each of the top three monotheistic religions, Christianity, Judaism, and Islam, recognize the existence of angels, they still convey the strong message that God is singular and all powerful, and that angels should not be worshipped.

Angel-like beings pop up in many other religions. Some appear with wings, others are celestial spirits, and a few are immortals who were once human and now aid others on to their next life.

In Zoroastrianism, there are three different angel-like beings with distinctive roles. The amesha spentas (Holy Immortals) are archangels who each have specific duties in relation to human life. The Yazataz (Adorable Ones) are in charge of the natural and spiritual world—governing the sun, moon, bodies of water, forests, and so forth. The Fravashis are similar to guardian angels. Each individual has a Fravashi, a guide and friend, who closely watches over them.

In Mahayana Buddhism, angel-like bodhisattvas teach and heal human beings but also provide rewards or carry out punishments. Bodhisattvas are compassionate beings who reside between heaven and earth, helping guide the spirits of the dead to be reincarnated. Kuan-yin is a well-known bodhisattva (viewed as both goddess and angel) of unconditional love, kindness, and mercy.

The Latin American religion Santeria includes a belief in Orishas, a type of guardian angel. Each is aligned with an element of nature and can be contacted through sacred rituals. Protection and knowledge of the future is said to be exchanged for a specific ritual or sacrifice. Orishas are immaterial beings who act as helpers to the Santerian god.

The Taoists Immortals attend to and worship a supreme deity. They are also demigods ministering spirits that teach, protect, heal, and perform miracles. The Immortals fly between worlds and deliver messages.

Native American–based shamanistic paths have spirits that deliver messages. Sometimes the spirit is that of a deceased loved one. Many of these come in the form of animals or birds. They might be seen as eagles, ravens, wolves, or bears.

In Wicca, there is a belief in "spirit guides" who sometimes take the form of an animal or just consist of raw energy. They send messages and protect. The Wiccan belief in spirit guides branches off native shamanism but is slightly altered. The spirit guides are said to be from nature, guiding and sending signals and messages directly through the psychic mind.

# RITUAL TO MEET YOUR GUARDIAN ANGEL

The purpose of this ritual is to align and mold your energy with that of your guardian angel. It's a ritual to acknowledge your guide's presence within your life as well as invite him or her to stick around!

**SUPPLIES:**

- a piece of cardboard (8 × 11 or smaller)
- a pair of scissors
- glue
- white craft feathers (as an alternative you can use white paint or correction fluid)
- twelve-inch-long white satin fabric cord (called rattail)
- an offering of thanks (dried flower, charm, poem, pretty ribbon, or coin)

Using the scissors and cardboard, cut out the basic shape of an angel: head, body, legs, and, of course, a pair of wings! Next, glue on craft feathers where its wings should be. If no craft fathers are available to you, you can paint on the cardboard with white paint or liquid correction fluid. Remember, the cardboard image doesn't have to be perfect—the goal is to make a simple angel representation.

While your art is drying, take the time to create or locate an offering. Offerings are given as a token of gratitude, so put your heart into the selection. Offerings of thanks include dried flowers, a poem you've written, a drawing, a pretty ribbon, or shiny coins. So long as it is meaningful, the possibilities for an offering are endless!

Once your angel has completely dried, gather the rest of your supplies: the pen, your offering, and the white satin (rattail) cord. You can perform the rest of this angel ritual within nature, your bedroom, or at the kitchen table. Just make sure you're comfortable and can grab yourself some time alone.

Hold the angel representation faceup in your palm. Visualize yourself in a white glowing light of energy; transfer that energy to your angel cutout. Say this chant three times:

> Angel, be in the light, shine little one bright.

Carefully write on the bottom of the angel representation the words "my guardian angel," along with the name that you have chosen for him or her. Then, carefully place the craft angel down.

Proceed to pick up the white cord and begin saying this affirmation:

> White feathered friend,
> My guardian angel watching
> I knot this cord to mold our energies!

Look to the angel representation and tie a knot each time the following poem requests, saying the rhyme aloud as you knot along the cord.

> With knot of one the process has begun,
> With know of two my words be true,
> With knot of three I make it be.

Tie the cord around the angel's midsection and finish up with this spoken phrase:

> I release my hesitations, free my mind, and open
> the pathways to my guardian.

The ritual is done; place the offering by the angel and keep in a special place. Record thoughts and experiences from this ritual on the next journal page provided.

# CHAPTER SEVEN

# Create Positive Rituals

## Acknowledge Inner Strength

A RITUAL IS A ceremony that conveys a specific goal or message. They aren't always religious, but they do encompass your mind, body, and soul. Rituals tap deep into our consciousness and awaken the stagnant energy within. The core purpose of a ritual is to evoke movement, change, and transformation.

When you perform a ritual, you are acknowledging and voicing a deep desire within your heart. By performing the ritual in chapter four, your need for closure was conveyed. In chapter five, you set aside your fear and put specific energies in motion to obtain your goals.

All rituals are important because they allow us to express ourselves in more ways. And when you feel you have no control, they are there to help you take that control back! Enacting a ritual is an action, a creation.

After you've performed any kind of ritual, it's a great idea to write on the journal page provided at the end of each chapter within this book. Jotting down your afterthoughts makes the ritual experience all the more complete. It's a final step in each chapter and the perfect expression of who you are at that very moment. Writing is therapeutic, and if the ritual got to your soul in such a way that it ached, then penning down those emotions can be very healing.

Last, rituals are a catalyst for self-improvement and internal awareness. During a ritual, lighting a candle isn't just a small action, it is lighting the path to a new beginning. Rubbing earth between your fingers isn't about getting dirty, it is molding your power with that of mother nature's. Rituals are a powerful source, an opening of your mind, and an expression of your heart. Enjoy all the beauty they have to offer!

##  Rituals—One Step Further

### Purifying the Ritual Area

At this point you've performed several ceremonies within nature, maybe in the confines of your bedroom, or perhaps sitting at the kitchen table. Atmosphere is important, but almost any mundane place can be transformed into ritual territory.

As I've mentioned, there is much more to rituals than what meets the eye. They give you inner power and strength through positive action. To immerse yourself completely in a ritual the next time you perform one, create a special place of power.

When it comes to working a ritual, privacy is highly important!

Unless you want another person to work with you (more on this later), it's best to politely request the time and space alone.

To create your place of power with a positive atmosphere, you'll want to cleanse the area before you set up. By cleansing, I am not talking about soap and water, I mean cleanse in the sense of filtering out negative energy and imbuing the area with a positive flow of power. This step is called purifying the ritual area.

All you'll need are good visualization skills and a stick of incense. Incense can be found at some health food stores, gift shops, dollar stores, and even at the mall. Ask around, and they will pop up everywhere.

To begin purifying the ritual space, light the incense and start walking around the area or room. Incense gives off a scent through a thin line of smoke. It is in touch with the element of air. Like air molecules, negative energy can't be seen, but if you've ever walked into a room and felt the air turn thick and uncomfortable, then you've sensed a buildup of negativity.

These unhealthy vibes can be cleansed easily! With the lighted incense stick, walk around the afflicted area and visualize negative energy as black smoke. The incense has white smoke so every time you move to a new section, visualize white incense smoke overtaking the black smoke. Positive flowing energy kicks out the bad stuff and revitalizes the space. Native Americans use incense-like sage bundles to "smudge" an area for purification. Incense sticks in place of sage bundles are an inexpensive substitute that produces a similar effect.

Purified areas make great places for ritual but also help when studying for a test or doing heavy mind work. After you've taken the incense around the ritual area, you can put it in a special incense holder to burn throughout your ritual or extinguish it for future use. At this time, you may gather all your supplies and start the ritual!

## Divine Assistance

To make your rituals more spiritually in tune, you might consider calling upon your guardian angel or asking for deity's guidance. Working with your guardian angel or specific higher power can create a loving bond. However, asking a divine being to watch over you during a ritual is completely optional. Give it a try if you feel the idea appeals to you or simply hold off until you're comfortable with the idea.

To request divine assistance, simply create a small spoken phrase as an invitation:

> *Angel of mine, be here with me*
> *So I may draw on your strength*
> *And bring forth a positive goal.*

Or,

> *Divine God (Goddess), send your rays of light my way,*
> *Help me achieve a greater good with this ritual.*

These invitations or similar ones you've written personally should be said after purifying the ritual space but before the actual ritual has begun.

## Rituals with a Friend

Almost all the rituals in this book are for solitary use because they are personal and require quiet space for concentration. However, a few of the rituals can be adapted for multiple practitioners. There is even one specifically for you and your good friend to work together at the end of this chapter!

Before you jump to these rituals with another person, there are a few things you should know ahead of time! When working with another, you'll want to prepare together and agree on the details beforehand. It's also important that both of you feel comfortable with the ritual—if not, take some time and revise it to your liking. Make initials next to every action, sectioning off who does what. Will both speak the chant or phrase in unison? Who lights the candle?

Next, add a little spunk to the atmosphere. Dress up in long scarves, costume jewelry, and funny outfits. Performing rituals together, especially ones for teen women, is a bonding experience. You're linking your soul to that of your friend, so make it memorable!

Last, do something celebratory afterward, like make ice cream sundaes, watch your favorite movie, or go out in nature. This is your time, your ritual, and sometimes it's best to let loose and have fun!

## ✳ Creating Your Own Rituals

Creating your own rituals is an interesting task, but it doesn't have to be a complicated one. If you thumb through this book, you may notice a few underlying themes—most prominent perhaps is the specific attention to atmosphere. Almost all the rituals request that you perform them in whole or in part within nature. It's all about feeling the power of mother earth course through your veins.

The items required are very easy to locate, as many tools can be found in or around the house. When creating your ritual, the atmosphere and easy access to supplies are key. But even before you start thinking about those things, the first step is defining your purpose or goal.

What is the purpose of your ritual? Is there something that you want to invite into your life? Banish away? Or even seek within yourself?

Many times simply acknowledging your desires sparks the flow of creativity and gets the ritual moving! Let's say you decided on a fun goal, like inviting good luck into your life. Everyone could use a little luck, right? Using this purpose as an example, we will work together and you'll learn how to create your own ritual.

To start, take a sheet of paper and jot down notes, notions, and feelings you associate with good luck. Maybe the colors green and gold come to mind? What about a small charm or pendant that you keep with you for good luck and positive energy?

Think of nature for a few moments: What items found in nature do you associate with luck? I immediately thought of dandelion seeds. Have you ever picked one up, made a wish, and then blown on it for good luck? Dandelions are seen as a weed, but in this case they are a useful tool in your ritual!

When I think of "good luck," our theme, I picture a leprechaun and pot of gold. Both of those elements are hard to come by. However, you might have gold craft sparkles around the house!

They can symbolically represent the pot of gold. A small piece of green cloth (fabric or felt) would fit into the color scheme, so it's a good item to have around. Let's compile a list of what we have so far: a favorite charm (or pendant), a dandelion, a dash of gold sparkles, and a small piece of green fabric. These tools have the possibility to work perfectly together!

Next, it's a good idea to get your goal out vocally, so let's create a small rhyme in conjunction with your effort! If you are not the rhyming type of woman, then a soft poem or well-written statement would do just fine.

Here is my example:

> Good luck come to me, around the sea
> Travel above, flow below
> Whisper wind, shiver tree
> Good luck come and stay with me!

Last, you'll pull your elements together and develop an action. What exactly will you do with the charm, dandelion, gold sparkles, and green cloth? Great question! Watch how all the pieces fall into place with this completed ritual.

## RITUAL FOR GOOD LUCK

The purpose of this ritual is to invite good luck into your life. The best moon phase for this ritual is new or waxing.

**SUPPLIES:**

> a personal charm (or pendant) that you keep for good luck and positive energy
>
> a dandelion
>
> a dash of gold sparkles
>
> a small piece of green fabric (cloth or felt)

Before you start, create a working area that's out of the way and will give you some privacy. Bring all of your supplies to the space. To add extra energy to a personal charm or pendant, wear the item during this ritual.

To begin, take the green cloth and lay it out before you. Visualize yourself in your protective light. Bring up images in your mind that you associate with luck. When you're done with that visualization, pick up your dandelion and say the following chant:

> Good luck come to me, around the sea
> Travel above, flow below
> Whisper wind, shiver tree
> Good luck come and stay with me!

Next, place the flower on top of the green cloth. Grab a dash of gold sparkles and lightly sprinkle them over your dandelion. Imagine yourself dancing in a stream of golden light. Feel the energy of good luck entering your soul and staying within your life.

*Carefully wrap the green cloth up around the flower and sparkles. Walk it outside and tuck it under a bush so that the item is somewhat hidden. Three days later, go to the charm and take back the green cloth. Leave the dandelion and sparkles as a gift. The leprechauns will send you good luck once the dandelion wilts.*

# Develop Your Own Ritual in Six Steps

This section works in conjunction with the previous section, Creating Your Own Rituals. It's a guide to help you develop your own rituals utilizing six simple steps!

1. Determine your goal for the ritual. Inviting? Banishing? Or seeking within?

2. Make notes. Think of possible items for your ritual. Look to nature, around the house, or pick up inexpensive items you know you can get your hands on.

3. Pick a time and place. Where is this ritual best performed? Is there a particular moon phase that you'd like to draw on? (See next page.)

4. Create a spoken phrase, statement, or affirmation that best suits your ritual goal. Remember, so long as it's meaningful, it doesn't have to rhyme!

5. Develop an action. How will you work with the tools you've chosen?

6. Pull all the elements together and write out your ritual.

## ✳ Moon Ritual Chart

| MOON PHASE | RITUAL THEMES |
| --- | --- |
| New Moon | Inner reflections, spiritual improvement, fresh starts, and new ventures.<br>Good for rituals of blessing, confidence, and self-love. |
| Waxing Moon | Draw in positive energy, invite growth, and build power.<br>Good for rituals of luck, happiness, healing, protection, and angel matters. |
| Full Moon | Multipurpose moon phase, peak of lunar energy and staying power.<br>Good for rituals of future aspiration, dream work, friendship, and all things Goddess! |
| Waning Moon | End, release, and cleanse.<br>Good for rituals of the soul, banishing anger, and burying the past. |

## RITUAL FOR SELF-LOVE

This particular ceremony reflects the notion and importance of self-love. Its healing energies are also helpful after the breakup of a relationship.

**SUPPLIES:**

> a bowl of water
>
> flower petals (or floating candles)
>
> a dash of cinnamon
>
> a mirror of any size

Gather all your supplies and find a quiet place. To begin, take a deep breath and visualize yourself in a white protection mist. If you'd like, call upon your guardian angel or the assistance of a deity.

Bring the bowl before you and start stirring the water with your index finger in a clockwise motion.

Cinnamon

Say the following rhyme while you continue to stir:

> **Water emotion,**
>
> **Intuitive force,**
>
> **My devotion,**
>
> **Power source.**

Next, sprinkle in a dash of cinnamon and pick up your mirror. Find your reflection and speak this affirmation aloud or in your mind:

> **I care**
>
> **I call**
>
> **Deep within my being**
>
> **Pride in who I am**
>
> **Loving tide ocean abundance**
>
> **Stay true**
>
> **Soul**
>
> **Be strong**
>
> **Spirit!**

One by one, drop a flower petal (or floating candle) into your water bowl. With each addition, speak this phrase:

> **Woman is beauty,**
>
> **I am woman.**

The ritual is done. You may want to write in a journal and express all your current emotions and insights. If you can, leave the water bowl in your room for two days, and each time you walk by stir with your index finger and reflect within.

## RITUAL OF FRIENDSHIP

The purpose of this two-part ritual is to keep an existing friendship strong. It's especially meaningful if you or your friend will be moving. For best results, work the ritual on or before the full moon.

**PART ONE**

**SUPPLIES:**

  embroidery floss
  scissors

The first half of this ritual asks you to create a friendship bracelet out of embroidery floss. When I was in fifth grade, making this type of bracelet became a big hobby! The weaving can be a simple braid or more intricate, but for this ritual it's the energy you put into your creation that makes the difference. Before you begin any work, you'll

want to determine with your friend which colors the bracelets will be composed of. Yellow and purple are the colors of friendship, but if you two share a favorite color scheme, work with that to make the friendship bracelets more personalized.

Once complete, the bracelet you make will be given to your friend and the one that she makes will belong to you! This part of the ritual requires some extra time if you've never worked with embroidery floss. In general, the floss should be cut to about eighteen inches in length, with several strands knotted together three inches in. After you have gotten your knot secured, start weaving! The pattern will shorten the length of the bracelet. Once both bracelets are complete, take a small break and prepare to start the second half of the ritual.

PART TWO

SUPPLIES:

a purple votive candle

a votive candle holder

matches or lighter

the friendship bracelets you both made (if you would like, matching scarves or necklaces can be substituted in place of the friendship bracelets)

To begin, gather your supplies, grab your friend, and find a quiet place to work. Place the purple candle in the votive holder and make sure it's in a safe place away from any flammable material. Carefully light the wick and sit cross-legged in front of your friend.

Say this chant together:

> **Here now, in this place**
> **Within this time, we bring about**
> **A friendship rhyme.**

Place your palms up to your friend's, so that they touch. Continue with this affirmation:

> **Friend to friend**
> **Palm to palm**
> **You and I come together**
> **May our friendship last forever.**

Next, put your hands down and find the friendship bracelet you made for your friend. Tie it on her wrist. Your friend should then return the gesture with the bracelet she made earlier. If you used the scarves as a replacement, put them in each other's hair or tie loosely around the neck.

Once you both are wearing the matching items, blow out the candle and clean up the ritual space. At this time, the ritual has been completed, but you may want to take the rest of your time together to do some friendship-bonding activities.

# Conclusion

WRITING *MOONBEANS & SHOOTING STARS* has been an amazing experience. I discovered hidden aspirations, reignited my passion for inner connectedness, and challenged myself beyond levels I could have imagined.

Finding the voice and tone came naturally because I pictured myself years ago, when I felt lost in my own life, and wrote for her. There were difficult chapters and frustrating days, but I embraced them and knew if I pushed passed the difficult phases I would persevere.

In many ways, my journey writing *Moonbeams* was parallel to my life—many good days and a few bad ones—but with a positive attitude and hard work, the end result was profoundly meaningful and intensely satisfying. I felt the guiding presence of a higher power and the comfort of angelic assistance.

My personal experiences were the foundation for much of my expression, but so was intuition. I can't stress enough the positive effects listening to intuition has on a person's soul. The two are bound together by some force of nature. Neither the soul nor intuition should be ignored; they are our divine gifts.

# Bibliography

Burnham, Sophy. *A Book of Angels: Reflections on Angels Past and Present and True Stories of How They Touch Our Lives.* New York: Ballantine, 1990.

Daniel, Alma, Timothy Wyllie, and Andrew Ramer. *Ask Your Angels.* New York: Ballantine, 1992.

Guiley, Rosemary Ellen. *An Angel in Your Pocket.* London: Thorsons, 1994.

Hamilton, Edith. *Mythology: Timeless Tales of Gods and Heroes.* New York: Warner, 1999.

Monaghan, Patricia. *The New Book of Goddesses and Heroines.* St. Paul, Minn.: Llewellyn, 1997.

Monaghan, Patricia. *Wild Girls: The Path of the Young Goddess.* St. Paul, Minn.: Llewellyn, 2001.

RavenWolf, Silver. *Angels: Companions in Magick.* St. Paul, Minn.: Llewellyn, 1996.

Stevenson, Jay. *The Complete Idiot's Guide to Angels.* New York: Alpha Books, 1998.

Tripp, Edward. *Crowell's Handbook of Classical Mythology.* New York: Thomas Y. Crowell, 1970.

# About the Author

Gwinevere Rain is a teen author who experiences life one step at a time, acknowledging the power of intuition and strong ethics as her guide. She follows a nature-based path and lives in rhythm with the moon.

Gwinevere's first book, *Spellcraft for Teens*, sparked her writing career and initiated her desire to show other young adults the power of inner magic. Her books emphasize the importance of inner connectedness, following dreams, as well as being tolerant of other faiths and lifestyles.

Gwinevere's hobbies include journaling, crafting jewelry, and working on her personal website, *www.Gothic-Rain.com*. She is currently writing her third book.

# About the Photography

The photography presented within this guide was a harmonious effort between Gwinevere and her mother, Ann. The images were achieved with Kodak 400-speed black-and-white film and a professional Pentax camera with a macro lens for close-up photography.

Gwinevere oversaw each photo session and incorporated her personal findings, belongings, and treasures within each shot. This unique endeavor between Gwinevere and her mother contributes to the positive energy and inspiration within this book.

Ann has a Bachelor of Science degree in graphic and fine art, and achieved her master's degree from Stonybrook University, Long Island.